The Secret of
SHARK
REEF

The three divers swam slowly down to the reef. Clutching his spear gun, Pete wondered if the others felt as nervous as he did. After all, they didn't call this Shark Reef for nothing!

The water was murky after the hurricane. But as Pete went deeper, he could see the sharp rock ridges of the reef more clearly. Suddenly he spied the very thing he dreaded—a shark! It was only fifty feet away and swimming slowly toward him.

Pete froze on the spot. Just don't panic, he said to himself. Whatever happens, don't panic!

Alfred Hitchcock

and The Three Investigators in——

The Secret of

SHARK REEF

——Text by William Arden

Based on characters created by Robert Arthur

Random House　New York

Library of Congress Cataloging in Publication Data
———.

Alfred Hitchcock and the three investigators in The Secret of Shark Reef.

(Alfred Hitchcock mystery series; no. 30)

Summary: Three young sleuths uncover a mystery buried since World War II when they come to the aid of a trouble-plagued environmentalist who is protesting the drilling of offshore oil wells.

[1. Mystery and detective stories] I. Arthur, Robert. II. Title III. Series.

PZ7.L984Ao   [Fic]   79–9925
ISBN 0–394–84249–9 pbk.   ISBN 0–394–94249–3 lib bdg.

Manufactured in the United States of America   9 0

Contents

Alfred Hitchcock
Warns the Fainthearted

Let all nervous readers beware! Do not turn
another page of this book unless you can face
wind and surging sea, sabotage and sharks, mud
slides and monstrous shapes that rise from the
ocean! Readers who lack the taste for breathless
adventure must seek out a tamer story!

But for stout-hearted readers who seek the
thrill of action, the latest deeds of The Three
Investigators will challenge mind and nerve!
Never have the junior detectives been caught up
in a wilder, more puzzling, more deadly series of
events. Each member of the intrepid trio is called
upon to outdo himself!

The ingenuity of the somewhat plump and
insufferably knowledgeable Jupiter Jones is
stretched to its utmost to solve mysteries that lead

only to more mysteries! The athletic prowess of Pete Crenshaw lets that tall, muscular boy go where the others dare not! And the quick thinking of studious Bob Andrews saves the day when all looks lost!

From the moment Bob's father invites the trio to accompany him to a new offshore oil-drilling platform, the boys are caught up in a whirlwind of mystery on land and sea! So, adventurous readers, turn the page and join our daring threesome as they seek out—and finally learn—the secret of Shark Reef!

ALFRED HITCHCOCK

The Secret of

SHARK REEF

Shark Reef #1!

"Shark Reef Number One?" Bob Andrews said. "Gosh, why do they call it that, Dad?"

Bob was standing next to his father in the plunging bow of a cabin cruiser. Also with him were his two best friends, Pete Crenshaw and Jupiter Jones. Pete looked nervously at the broad blue ocean all around them, and at the mountainous islands looming ahead.

"Shark Reef Number One sure doesn't sound friendly!" Pete said.

Mr. Andrews laughed. "Most oil-drilling platforms are named, boys. This new platform is about half a mile from a famous reef called Shark Reef, and it's the first platform on the spot, so—Shark Reef Number One." Mr. Andrews' eyes twinkled mischievously. "Many ships were wrecked on the reef in the old days, but that hasn't happened in a long time. Of course, the

3

reef got its name from the sharks that live on it. They're still around."

Pete groaned. "I knew it wasn't a friendly name!"

The fourth member of the quartet in the bow, stocky Jupiter Jones, stood peering ahead at the towering islands to the south. They sheltered the expanse of blue water known as the Santa Barbara Channel, which the cabin cruiser was now crossing. The three largest islands—Santa Cruz, Santa Rosa, and San Miguel—seemed to be a single land mass like another mainland, with a wide gap between them and the smaller Anacapa Island to the east. It was toward this gap that the speeding boat plunged.

"Not long now!" Jupiter exclaimed as the boat began to round the tip of Santa Cruz Island. It was Jupiter who had been the most excited when Mr. Andrews had offered to take the boys with him early that June afternoon.

The three boys, known in their home town of Rocky Beach, California, as the junior detective team of The Three Investigators, had been lazing around Bob's backyard when Mr. Andrews suddenly came out of the house.

"Boys," Mr. Andrews called, "how would you like to come on an interesting adventure with me?"

"What adventure, Mr. Andrews?" Pete exclaimed.

"There's a new oil platform in the ocean off Santa Barbara," Mr. Andrews said, "and the environmentalists are trying to prevent the oil men from starting to drill. My paper wants me to write a story on it."

Mr. Andrews worked as a reporter for a Los Angeles newspaper, and was occasionally sent out of town to cover events.

"Gosh, Dad," Bob said, "there are a lot of platforms out there already. What's so special about this one?"

"I know!" Jupiter broke in eagerly. "It was on TV last night. The new platform is the first outside the Channel Islands. It's the start of a whole new oil field very close to the islands, and the environmental people are outraged! Those islands are still almost untouched and are full of birds, animals, plants, and marine life. An oil spill could destroy them!"

Mr. Andrews nodded. "Protesters tried to prevent the platform's even being erected by sailing boats all over the spot."

"And now," Jupiter added, "there are hundreds of boats out there circling around and trying to stop the drilling from starting! When would we go up there, Mr. Andrews?"

"Right now," Mr. Andrews said, "if your families agree."

Pete and Jupe immediately biked home to get permission and pack a bag. In no time they had rejoined Bob and Mr. Andrews for the eighty-mile drive north. Several hours later, after leaving their bags at a motel, they stood in the bow of the cabin cruiser as it sailed out of Santa Barbara harbor.

In the broad channel, many oil-drilling platforms stood between the city of Santa Barbara and the islands. Rising high out of the sea, with their derricks set on one side, they looked like a fleet of aircraft carriers. Pete studied them.

"Wasn't this where all the big trouble about oil spills from ocean drilling started?" the tall boy asked.

"Yes," Jupiter said, and began to pull facts out of his encyclopedic memory. "The city of Santa Barbara tried to stop oil drilling out here because of the earthquakes and the danger to the beaches and marine life, but the government let the oil companies go ahead. Then in January 1969 a well blew out of control. Before it was contained, at least 235,000 gallons of oil had spilled into the ocean! The oil made an incredible mess, and killed a lot of wildlife."

Pete stared. "Then why are all these platforms still here? Shouldn't they be taken out?"

"A lot of people think so," Mr. Andrews answered. "But it's not an easy decision, Pete. The country needs all the oil it can get to keep everything running and make all the things we need. But we also have to protect the environment, and maybe that's more important than the oil."

The cruiser heaved across the waves and currents of the channel, and finally rounded the eastern end of towering Santa Cruz Island into the open ocean.

"There it is!" Jupiter pointed ahead to the west.

"Shark Reef Number One!" Bob exclaimed.

Jutting out of the sea on its great steel legs, the new oil-drilling platform looked like some solitary metal monster ready to walk all the way to Japan. As the cabin cruiser drew nearer, the Investigators could make out the parts of the platform. It consisted of several layers of deck, some partly enclosed, built out over the enormously thick legs. On the top deck, a tall crane and an even taller drilling derrick rose high in the air. The whole construction was enormous. Jupiter estimated that the platform was about 100 feet long on each side, and that the top of the derrick was about 150 feet above the sea. The platform dwarfed the flotilla of boats around it, gleaming in the late-afternoon sun.

"Wow!" Pete gasped. "There must be a hundred of them!"

Boats of every description had shown up for the protest. There were private cabin cruisers of all types, tall sailboats, smaller catamarans, elegant semi-yachts, rusty old fishing boats, sleek and fast deep-sea charter fishing boats, powerful work boats of the type used by the oil companies themselves, and even one enormous real yacht. They were all sailing in a wide circle around the platform like Indians attacking a frontier fort.

Banners with messages of protest flew from all the masts. As Mr. Andrews and the boys sailed closer, they could hear chanting over loudspeakers and bull horns that grew louder and louder: ". . . Get oil out! . . . Get oil out! . . . Polluters go home! . . . Save the birds, save the sea, save us all! . . . Heck no, oil must go! . . . Hey, hey, wha'd'ya say! How much oil will you spill today! . . ."

A black fishing boat with a flying bridge broke from the circle and sailed in closer to the platform. Two men stood on the bridge, which was actually the flat roof of the boat's cabin. One man was at the wheel, and the second stood braced against the railing that ran around the roof. Both men were yelling taunts at the oil-rig workers on the platform high above them. The oil men were angrily shouting back at the protesters: ". . . Stay away from this rig! . . . Why don't you all go fishing? . . . You want horses back? . . . What do you think your boats run on? . . . Blasted radicals! . . ."

A long work boat that sailed alone inside the circle herded the breakaway boat back into line. Lean and powerful, the work boat carried the name *Sea Wind* on its wheelhouse and stern. A banner on its low cabin proclaimed: SAVE THE ISLANDS COMMITTEE. Mr. Andrews told the cruiser captain to sail through the circle and up to it.

"Committee boat!" he shouted. "Bill Andrews from the press!"

On the *Sea Wind,* a tall man with a thin face and horn-rimmed glasses looked around at them. He wore a heavy turtleneck sweater, and his long brown hair blew in the wind. He took a black pipe out of his mouth and raised a bull horn. "Hello! Come alongside!"

Crewmen on both boats heaved and tied lines, and soon the boats bobbed side by side in the ocean swell. The tall man came to the rail and nodded to Mr. Andrews and the boys.

"Glad you wanted to come up, Andrews. Now you can see just what an outrage this platform is! Open to any storm, flanked by dangerous reefs that could break a tanker in half, and almost on top of the islands!"

"I'll get the facts, Crowe," Mr. Andrews said, and turned to the boys with a sudden grin. "Boys, I have a surprise—a bonus for coming with me. Meet Mr. John Crowe, the famous author!"

"John Crowe, the mystery writer!" Bob cried.

"Wow," Pete exclaimed, "I've read all your books!"

"We all have!" Jupiter echoed. "Are you out here gathering material for a mystery novel, Mr. Crowe?"

"No," the author said. "I'm chairman of the committee against this platform. Protecting the environment is everyone's job, even if we have to put aside our own work for a time."

He glared at the steel platform rising out of the sea,

then suddenly smiled. "Besides, I'm not the only famous one here, am I? When Andrews told me he might bring along his son, Bob, Pete Crenshaw, and Jupiter Jones, he should have said he was bringing The Three Investigators!"

"You know about us!" the three boys cried at once.

"I've read many of your cases," Mr. Crowe said, "and I've always meant to ask you for a special favor. May I have one of your famous cards for my collection of mystery mementos?"

Bob and Pete beamed proudly as Jupiter solemnly handed one of the Investigators' business cards across the boat railings to Mr. Crowe. It read:

THE THREE INVESTIGATORS
"We Investigate Anything"
? ? ?

First Investigator . . . . Jupiter Jones
Second Investigator . . . . . . Peter Crenshaw
Records and Research . . . . . . Bob Andrews

A bearded man wearing an old Navy officer's cap and a heavy pea jacket came hurrying up. His wind-burned and weathered face was troubled, and his dark eyes were angry. He muttered something to Mr. Crowe. The author nodded grimly.

"This is Captain Jason. He owns the *Sea Wind*. I'm afraid we'll have to postpone any further—" Mr.

Crowe suddenly stopped. He stared thoughtfully down at the card in his hand, then looked at the Investigators.

"Boys," he said slowly, "you may have arrived just in time. I think I have a mystery for you to solve!"

2

A Puzzling Loss

"Gosh," Pete said, "you're a mystery writer, Mr. Crowe. Why don't you just solve the mystery yourself?"

"Apparently, Pete, there is a difference between being a detective writer and being a real detective," Mr. Crowe said drily. "I have to admit that the problem has me thoroughly stumped. But The Three Investigators are real detectives, right?"

Jupe nodded. "We'll be glad to help," he said, just a little smugly. "If you can tell us exactly what . . ."

Captain Jason of the *Sea Wind* looked at his watch nervously. "There isn't much time, Mr. Crowe."

"All right, Captain," Crowe said. "As I started to tell you earlier, boys, we must go back to shore at once. As a matter of fact, that *is* the mystery, but I'm afraid we'll have to put off discussing it until we can meet onshore."

"Unless the boys go back with you," Mr. Andrews suggested. "I'll be taping interviews with protesters on the other boats, and don't really need them with me."

"That would be perfect!" Crowe exclaimed. "I could fill them in while we sail back."

"You're sure it's all right, Dad?" Bob asked eagerly.

Mr. Andrews nodded. "Crowe's mystery, whatever it is, might even be part of the protest story. So go on, over the rail with the three of you. I'll join you later at Mr. Crowe's house, and you can give me a full report."

With the help of Captain Jason and the captain of the cabin cruiser, the boys climbed over the railings in the rolling swell and onto the deck of the *Sea Wind*. The two boats cast off from each other, and the cabin cruiser turned to join the circle of protest boats, where Mr. Andrews would conduct his on-the-spot interviews.

Over the *Sea Wind*'s radio, Mr. Crowe called his assistant chairman on another boat. He instructed him to take over the lead-boat position, and the *Sea Wind* headed for home, a little more than an hour away. Fast and powerful, it quickly left the other boats and the towering oil platform behind as it plunged toward the broad gap between Santa Cruz and Anacapa islands.

"There's another boat going in," Bob said, pointing ahead.

Still flying its banners of protest, the other boat was some miles ahead. It was the black boat with the flying bridge that had strayed from the circle. It was already at the gap and turning into the Santa Barbara Channel.

"Those Connors brothers!" Mr. Crowe said, shading his eyes to stare ahead. "Abalone divers from Oxnard. They volunteered to join the protest, but I'm not sure I should have let them. They don't take to organization very well. We're all supposed to arrive at the platform together and leave together. The protest carries more impact that way."

"Then why are we leaving early, Mr. Crowe?" Peter wondered.

"Because we have to, Pete," Mr. Crowe said grimly. "We don't have enough fuel left to stay out here any longer. And that, boys, is the mystery!"

"*What* is the mystery, Mr. Crowe?" Bob asked, wiping salt spray off his glasses.

"Why, for the fourth time in a week, the *Sea Wind* hasn't had enough fuel to remain at sea the full twelve hours we try to keep up the protest!"

"But"—Jupiter frowned—"couldn't you just plan the time out here to fit your fuel capacity?"

"We did, Jupiter," Mr. Crowe said. "The *Sea Wind* is a fast, powerful craft, which is why I hired it as the

lead boat. It consumes a great deal of fuel, but
Captain Jason calculated that with full tanks we could
be at sea twelve hours. Therefore we planned for
precisely twelve hours harbor to harbor, but three
times this week we had only enough fuel for ten or
eleven hours, and the same thing has just happened
again today!"

"You're sure you started out with full tanks?" Pete
asked.

"Absolutely. We even measured with a stick
gauge."

"And," Jupiter said slowly, "the mystery is, what
happened to the lost fuel?"

"Exactly."

The *Sea Wind* had passed between Santa Cruz and
Anacapa islands now, and was speeding northwest
through the calmer seas of the broad Santa Barbara
Channel. Ahead, the black boat was still over a mile
in the lead.

"Is it always the same?" Jupiter asked after a time.
"I mean, is the same amount of fuel missing each
time?"

"Yes and no, and that's a mystery too," Mr. Crowe
said. "Each time we've had to go in, the fuel gauge
showed the same low reading. But the first time we
made it back to Santa Barbara with a few gallons to
spare, as Captain Jason calculated we would, and the
next two times we ran dry a mile or so offshore and

had to radio for a tow! This time we have some extra fuel in cans just in case."

"Sir," Bob said, "did you check the tides?"

"Yes, Bob. Captain Jason did that at once. There was nothing unusual, nothing he hadn't calculated in his fuel-need figures."

"What about winds and currents?" Pete said.

"All normal for this time of year. There's a big storm down off Baja California in Mexico, but no effects have reached here yet."

"Could something be wrong with the engine?" Bob suggested.

"Or your fuel gauge?" Pete added.

Mr. Crowe shook his head. "Those were our first thoughts. But the engine checks out perfectly, and so does the fuel gauge. There are no leaks in the fuel tanks or lines, either, and the propeller and shaft are normal."

"Then there's only one possible answer," Bob said. "Someone is stealing the fuel!"

"Sure!" Pete echoed. "It has to be that."

"For the last three days," Mr. Crowe said, "Captain Jason and my gardener have watched the boat all night. No one has come near it! Not anyone they could see, anyway."

Jupiter had been silent while Bob and Pete suggested answers, his plump face deep in thought. Now he looked out at the channel without seeming to notice the speed of the boat or the islands receding behind them.

"Is the *Sea Wind* the only boat this has happened to, Mr. Crowe?" the leader of the trio asked slowly.

"Yes, Jupiter," Mr. Crowe said. "And that makes it even more mysterious. I admit I am completely baffled, but I'm convinced of one thing—it isn't any accident!"

Pete gulped. "You mean you think someone is . . . sabotaging the *Sea Wind?*"

"Like the oil company that built Shark Reef Number One?" Bob added.

"*Someone* is doing it," Mr. Crowe said, "but for the life of me I can't see how or even why."

The *Sea Wind* had come rapidly closer to the mainland as they talked. They could see Santa Barbara harbor not more than a mile ahead when Captain Jason came up to them.

"Almost out of fuel again!" the bearded captain reported angrily. "Just like the last two times."

"But not," Jupiter said with a thoughtful frown, "like the first time."

"You think that's important, Jupiter?" Mr. Crowe said.

"It could be, sir. Anything *different* is important in a mystery."

Captain Jason went off to put the emergency fuel into the tanks. The boys and Mr. Crowe puzzled over the mystery of the missing fuel as the *Sea Wind* headed in to Santa Barbara harbor.

The harbor was bounded by land on the northern and western sides. The southern side was a stone breakwater, and a long oil-company wharf jutted into the sea to form the eastern side. Between the breakwater and the wharf was the harbor entrance, which a sand bar was always trying to close. The *Sea Wind* had to slow almost to a stop to pass through the narrow channel that had been dredged in the sand bar.

To the left of the harbor entrance, the sand bar rose above water to make a long, narrow beach that reached to the outer end of the breakwater. Open to the best waves of the channel, the sand-bar beach swarmed with surfers in black wetsuits. They hurried in and out of the surf with their long boards.

Once inside the harbor, the *Sea Wind* headed for the marina. It was built along the concrete sea wall that shored up the harbor's western side.

"My car is in the marina parking lot," Mr. Crowe said as the *Sea Wind* glided past wooden docks into its berth against the sea wall. "But first I want to check out the people we have picketing on the oil-company wharf."

Leaving Captain Jason to secure the *Sea Wind* for the night, the others climbed ashore and hurried toward the wide promenade at the northern end of the harbor. It bordered a second beach—the harbor beach—which ran between the marina and the oil-company wharf. Now, in the early evening, the promenade was thronged with boaters, tourists, surfers and skin divers in wetsuits, and bathers leaving the harbor beach. Suddenly the Investigators became aware that many of the people were hurrying toward the oil-company wharf. An angry roar came from the wharf—the roar of many voices chanting in unison.

"No way, go away! . . . No way, go away! . . . No way, go away!"

Mr. Crowe looked alarmed. He started to run.

"Something's wrong at the wharf! Hurry, boys!"

3

An Angry
Confrontation

An anxious Mr. Crowe led the boys forward. Ahead of them State Street, the main street of Santa Barbara, crossed the shoreline boulevard and met the oil-company wharf. Three large trucks piled high with drilling pipe were lined up before the entrance to the wharf, their drivers and workmen staring ahead. At the wharf entrance itself a knot of protesters with placards and banners blocked the way.

"Something is wrong!" Mr. Crowe exclaimed. "The oil-company manager and I agreed to have no confrontations while the courts were deciding if drilling could start!"

"Look, sir!" Jupiter pointed. "I think there's the reason for the trouble!"

In the open space between the trucks and the pickets, a long black limousine was parked. Some ten feet in front of it, a broad-shouldered man wearing a vested suit and a yellow hard hat angrily faced the line of protesters.

"I'm warning you crazy do-gooders for the last time! Get out of my way! I've got oil to produce, and I don't care about a few lousy fish!"

"Crowe said we had an agreement!" someone shouted.

"He said we had a truce!"

The man in the hard hat sneered. "I don't deal with radicals! Now I want you all . . ."

Among the pickets a rough-looking man in dirty overalls, rubber boots, and a wetsuit top pushed to the front. He had a broad, wind-reddened face and wore a black wool hat.

"And *we* don't deal with business crooks!" he snarled.

Behind him another heavyset man, dressed identically except for a bright red wool hat, pushed to the front and turned to face the other pickets. He waved his arms fiercely.

"This guy's not keeping any truce! I say no pipe on this pier! No pipe, no drilling! No way, go away!"

All the pickets linked arms and took up the chant.

"No way, go away! . . . No way, go away! . . ."

The businessman in the hard hat flushed.

"We're coming through!" he cried. "Easy or hard, it's up to you!"

The protester in the black wool hat shouted, "Sit down! Front row sit down right where you are!"

The oil man in the yellow hard hat waved to his truckdrivers and workers. They began to mass behind him.

Mr. Crowe and the boys reached the trucks. A short, slender man in his thirties wearing a windbreaker and chino pants jumped down from the first truck. He joined Mr. Crowe and the boys as they hurried toward the sitting pickets.

"Those two in the boots got them to block our trucks, Crowe," the newcomer said. "We made a deal, I thought."

"Who are they?" Jupiter asked, puffing.

"The Connors brothers. The abalone divers who have that black boat with the flying bridge," Mr. Crowe said. "Jed in the black wool hat, and Tim in the red." He nodded at the slender man trotting with them. "This is Mr. Paul MacGruder, boys, manager of the oil company here in Santa Barbara. And our deal didn't include truckloads of pipe, MacGruder!"

"I know that," Paul MacGruder acknowledged, "and I'm sorry about it. We're only going to store it on the wharf for now, but I was against bringing it in anyway. Mr. Hanley there insisted."

"Who is Mr. Hanley?" Crowe snapped as they reached the menacing gang of oil workers. The leader in the yellow hard hat turned around and glared at Crowe's party.

"Mr. Hanley," MacGruder said, "this is John Crowe, chairman of the protest committee. Mr. Hanley is—"

"I'm president of this oil company," Mr. Hanley snapped. "And if you can't control your people, Crowe, I will!"

"This is a public street, Mr. Hanley," Crowe said bluntly, "and your belligerent attitude isn't helping things."

"I won't be pushed around by a pack of freaks!" Mr. Hanley raged. "I say you're trespassing, and you're probably behind the sabotage out on the platform!"

"Sabotage?" Crowe said. "We haven't gone near—"

"Someone's been destroying equipment on Shark Reef Number One! Who goes out there except your boats?"

MacGruder said, "Mr. Hanley, we don't really need the pipe here yet. Maybe we should just send it back."

"I'm putting that pipe on our wharf!" Hanley roared. "You want Mr. Yamura to return to Japan and report that we can't run our business in this country?" He nodded toward a bald little man in a gray silk suit who was standing quietly by the limousine and its chauffeur. The man, who looked about sixty, nodded politely in return and continued to watch the scene through his steel-rimmed glasses.

Mr. Crowe was angry. "If you want to talk about sabotage, someone is tampering with my boat! Four times now we haven't had enough fuel to get back to harbor! From now on my man Torao will be on guard at the boat every second when I'm not!"

"I don't care if the F.B.I. guards your boat," Mr. Hanley said nastily. "Get your people out of my way, or my men will do it for you!"

At that, the oil workers began to hurl taunts at the protesters. Tim Connors picked up a length of two-by-four from the edge of the wharf.

"Grab a weapon!" he yelled. "We'll fight 'em!"

The oil workers began to move forward. The protesters who had been sitting leaped up and stood fast. Jed Connors suddenly swore. He charged toward the oil men, and his brother came right behind him. Two big oil men jumped forward to meet them.

Suddenly sirens began to wail in the distance from three directions. They came rapidly closer. Mr. Hanley swore.

"Who the devil called the police?"

MacGruder said, "I did. Ten minutes ago."

"Who are you working for, MacGruder?" Hanley demanded. "I want no weak sisters working with me! Don't you want this protesting stopped?"

"Not by this kind of violence," MacGruder said.

Before the oil-company president could answer, the whole roadway had erupted into a wild melee! The Connors brothers grappled with the two oil men, and the rest of the oil workers and protesters surged together. Then the police were all around, pushing between the combatants and separating them. In fifteen minutes it was all over.

An older policeman with gold braid on his cap came up to Crowe. "How did this get started, John?" he asked sharply.

"The president of the oil company tried to push three loads of pipe onto the wharf, Max! His limousine is over—"

Crowe turned toward where the limousine had been parked. It was gone. So were Hanley, Yamura, and the chauffeur.

"The oil workers say a pair of hotheads among your pickets started it," the policeman named Max said. "You'd better point them out."

"Gosh," Pete said, "I don't see them, Mr. Crowe!"

"They're gone, too!" Bob cried.

"And so is Mr. MacGruder," Jupiter added.

Crowe nodded slowly. "Max, these three boys are The Three Investigators, a junior detective team from down in Rocky Beach. Boys, this is Captain Max Berg of our police department."

"The Three Investigators?" Captain Berg smiled. "I've heard of you from Chief Reynolds in Rocky Beach. He thinks a lot of you."

The three boys beamed.

"That Hanley provoked my people," Crowe said to the captain, "but we shouldn't have gotten out of hand. I'll have to talk to the committee about restraining the hotheads."

"All right, John," the captain said. "We won't make any arrests this time. I'll send the trucks away, send your pickets home, and post a police guard here. You can all take a day to cool off."

Crowe thanked the captain, and led the boys back to the marina parking lot. The boys piled into Crowe's battered old Buick station wagon.

"Sir," Jupiter said as they drove away from the harbor, "it almost seemed as if those Connors brothers were purposely stirring up your pickets. As if they wanted the police to come, and perhaps ban the protest."

"They did come in early from the platform," Bob added.

"And," Jupiter went on, "that could be the reason behind your fuel loss—to discredit you and discourage the other protesters by making the committee boat leave the protest early so many times."

"You mean the Connors brothers could be working for the oil company?" Mr. Crowe asked. "Trying to make us look violent?"

Jupiter nodded. "It's an old trick, sir."

"I don't know, First," Pete objected. "It didn't look like that Mr. Hanley needed much help to stir up trouble. Maybe *he's* trying to discredit Mr. Crowe by swiping the fuel."

"Perhaps," Jupiter answered as Mr. Crowe turned into the driveway of a large old house on the upper east side of the city.

It was a neighborhood of big old frame houses, mostly renovated, with well-cared-for lawns and bright flower gardens. But Mr. Crowe's house was not renovated. Sprawling and ramshackle, it was surrounded by old trees and rose gardens. There was no lawn at all.

Jupiter seemed too busy thinking to even notice the house as they all got out of the Buick. "Mr. MacGruder," the stout Investigator mused, "seems to want to prevent any trouble at all. He's trying to keep everything calm."

"So am I, Jupiter," Mr. Crowe said. "Violence never helps."

"No, sir," Jupiter agreed, "but I wonder if Mr. MacGruder could have some special reason for wanting nothing to change."

"He's sure taking a risk opposing Mr. Hanley," Bob said.

They were walking toward the front door when there was suddenly a loud crash at the rear.

"What in—?" Mr. Crowe began.

Someone ran noisily behind the old house.

"Around in the back!" Pete cried, leading the way.

They all dashed around the house. In the backyard was a small lemon orchard, reaching from the house to a rear fence.

A figure in a black wetsuit was running through the orchard. He scrambled over the fence and was gone!

4

A Curious Intruder

"Look!" Bob cried. "The back window!"

A rear window of the big house was open. Directly under it, a garbage can lay knocked over.

"He was in the house!" Jupiter said. "We must catch him!"

Mr. Crowe nodded quickly. "There's an alley on the other side of the back fence—he's probably escaping that way. Pete and Bob, run back to the street and circle around left and right to head him off at either end of the alley! Jupe and I'll go after him!"

Bob and Pete vanished around the house as Mr. Crowe ran through the orchard with Jupiter behind him. The author vaulted the fence. Jupiter scrambled up after him and sprawled on the ground on the other side. Red-faced, the plump Investigator got up quickly and followed Mr. Crowe out into the alley. They looked both ways.

"He's gone!" the author fumed.

Bob and Pete appeared at the ends of the alley. Both waved and shook their heads. They had not seen the intruder!

"He must have run through the next yard to the next street," Mr. Crowe decided. He waved Bob and Pete on to the street ahead.

With Jupiter puffing behind, Mr. Crowe ran across the alley and through the nearest yard. They passed another big house, and came out into the street beyond.

Pete stood at the left corner and Bob at the right corner. No one else was in sight.

"We . . . we lost him!" Jupiter panted.

Mr. Crowe nodded bleakly as Bob and Pete trotted up to join them. Pete's face was confused.

"We didn't see any cars drive away from the alley or from this street," he said. "How did he get away?"

"He must have doubled back and fooled us," Jupiter concluded. "Or he's hiding. We won't find him now."

Dejected, they returned to Crowe's house through the yards.

"He had a wetsuit on," Bob said. "Those Connors brothers were wearing wetsuit tops at the wharf!"

"Santa Barbara is full of people in wetsuits," Mr.

Crowe said. "I have one myself."

They were walking through the orchard in Mr. Crowe's backyard when Pete suddenly froze.

"Someone's hiding over there," he whispered.

He pointed to a corner of the house, where a shadowy figure was bent low behind some camellia bushes. Mr. Crowe laughed.

"It's Torao, my new gardener. I didn't know he'd arrived. Perhaps he saw the intruder!"

They hurried over to the gardener, who was carefully feeding the camellia bushes. He was a small, slim Japanese youth in his late teens or early twenties. He wore only a T-shirt, shorts, and sandals.

"Hello, Torao," Mr. Crowe said.

The gardener looked up, startled. He had been so engrossed in his work that he had not heard them approach. He grinned and nodded, but did not speak.

"Have you been here long, Torao?" Mr. Crowe asked.

"Just come," the small youth said.

"Did you see anyone around the house? In a wetsuit?"

"Not see one." Torao shook his head.

"You didn't hear us chasing him?" Jupiter asked.

Torao blinked. "Just come. Not hear."

His voice was pleasant but nervous, as if he was uneasy in a strange country. He smiled, but he seemed confused.

"All right, Torao," Mr. Crowe said. "Oh, by the way, can you watch the *Sea Wind* again tonight for me?"

"Watch?" Torao frowned, then understood. "Ah, yes, can do."

"All right, then," Mr. Crowe said, and turned to the boys. "Now let's find out what my visitor was up to, if we can."

As they started for the door, Torao suddenly spoke again.

"See *two* men," he said eagerly. "Stand at corner."

"What did they look like, Torao?" Jupiter asked quickly.

The young gardener looked at Crowe unhappily.

"His English isn't good enough, Jupiter," Mr. Crowe said. "I'm afraid that's all he can tell us."

Mr. Crowe led the boys into the house, to the room where the intruder had left the window open. It was Mr. Crowe's study—a small room with a desk piled with books, notes, a finished manuscript, rows of colored pens, and an old manual typewriter. The study also had a canvas director's chair, an old stereo, and three battered filing cabinets. In a corner was a large ship-to-shore radio transmitter/receiver.

The top drawer of one filing cabinet was ajar. A notebook was open on top of the cabinet next to a large map. Mr. Crowe stared down at the notebook.

"What did he want with my committee book?"

Pete picked up the map. "Hey, this is a chart of the reefs and water depths around the islands."

"Anyone can get that chart," Mr. Crowe said, mystified.

Jupiter looked at the chart. "Perhaps not with the new platform and your route out to it drawn in. Just what is in the notebook, sir?"

"My daily schedule for our protest—what we will do each day at the rig and onshore, when we'll go out and return, what boats are available, who will go where, all that."

"Has this ever happened before?" Jupiter said. "I mean, someone coming in and reading the note-book?"

Mr. Crowe thought. "Possibly, Jupiter. I never saw anyone, but sometimes I've had the feeling that the book had been moved. I didn't think anything of it, but now—"

A knock at the study door stopped him. Torao looked in.

"Man come," the small gardener said.

Mr. Andrews strode into the room. "Well, is the mystery all solved?"

"I'm afraid," Mr. Crowe said, "that all we've done is find a few more mysteries. I hope you did somewhat better."

"Yes, I had some fine interviews with your people. Got some good stuff on tape. Now I'll interview the oil-company representatives. You boys care to come along?"

"Why not, Dad." Bob sighed. "We're not doing much good here."

"We could even stop for dinner, maybe?" Pete suggested.

Mr. Andrews laughed. "I expect that can be arranged. Care to join us for dinner, Crowe?"

"I'd better not leave here. There's something funny going on. I just wish I knew what and why."

Jupiter still held the notebook. He was staring down at the chart of the reefs and islands.

"Mr. Crowe," he said, "do you have a log for the *Sea Wind*?"

"Captain Jason does. He's probably still on the boat."

"Then," Jupiter said, "I'll decline the invitation to go to the oil-company interviews. I'd prefer to return to our motel room, if you wouldn't mind stopping a moment at the *Sea Wind* first, Mr. Andrews."

"Jupe!" Bob and Pete cried in unison. "You have an idea?"

"Perhaps," Jupiter said maddeningly.

"You'll skip dinner too, Jupiter?" Mr. Andrews said.

"Well," Jupiter said hastily, "I might just manage some dinner."

Everyone in the small study laughed.

5

Unexpected
Visitors

It was dark when Pete, Bob, and Mr. Andrews
returned to the motel on State Street where they had
dropped Jupiter after dinner. They found him sitting
at the desk in one of their two rooms. The logbook of
the *Sea Wind*, Mr. Crowe's notebook, and the chart of
the islands were spread out in front of him.

"Boy," Pete said as he collapsed into a chair, "I
never knew interviewing was such hard work!"

"They talk about everything except what you want
to hear!" Bob agreed. "It's sure tough to get the real
facts."

Mr. Andrews laughed. "Part of the job, boys.
Sometimes you get a better story by letting people
talk about whatever they want. They reveal what they
really are, how they *really* think."

"Then that Mr. Hanley sure doesn't care about

34

birds or fish," Pete said, "and he hates conservation-ists."

"He doesn't care what happens to the rest of the world," Bob added, "as long as his company sells a lot of gasoline."

"He and Mr. Yamura have a different view of what is good for the world, Bob," Mr. Andrews explained. "And they're right about all the people who wouldn't have jobs if we didn't have oil. Right now, the world does need a lot of oil."

Jupiter turned at the desk. "Just who is Mr. Yamura, sir?"

"A Japanese industrialist over here to consult with the oil company, Jupiter. It seems his family has owned an oil and chemical company in Japan for years."

"Maybe he can teach Mr. Hanley something," Bob said.

"The Japanese are no better about conservation than Hanley," Mr. Andrews said. He looked at his watch. "I still have to interview that local manager, MacGruder. His office said he might be at the wharf. If you all want to come along again, maybe we could stop for some ice cream, eh?"

Pete grinned. "That sounds good to me."

Jupiter stood up. "Unfortunately, we promised Mr. Crowe we'd go back to his house tonight."

"We did?" Bob said.

"Gosh, Jupe, I don't—" Pete began, then grunted as Bob kicked him. "Ow! Oh yeah, I remember now. We said we'd go back later tonight to . . . to . . ."

"Plan what we'll do tomorrow," Jupiter said.

"Well, then," Mr. Andrews said, "I'll look for MacGruder myself, and if I can't find him I'll drop in at the *Sun-Press*—the local paper—to look over their photos. I won't be late, and don't you boys be. We have a long day tomorrow."

The moment Mr. Andrews had gone, Pete bent to rub his ankle where Bob had kicked him, and complained loudly.

"You didn't have to kick so hard! I don't remember anyone saying we had to go back to Mr. Crowe's to do—"

"Pete!" Bob cried. "Jupe's solved the mystery! Right, Jupe?"

"I think so, yes," Jupiter answered somewhat smugly. "Or most of it, at least. The solution's there in the *Sea Wind*'s logbook. With the log, and what we already know, I think I can tell Mr. Crowe exactly what happened to his fuel!"

"Tell *us!*" the other two cried.

Jupiter grinned. "When we get there."

Bob and Pete groaned, but helped Jupiter gather up the logbook, notebook, and map and followed him out of the motel. In the quiet night they walked across State Street toward Mr. Crowe's house, only a few blocks away on Garden Street. The author himself let them in, and they went into his cluttered study again. On the short-wave marine radio in the corner, the Coast Guard was reporting on a hurricane now moving north.

"Boys, I didn't expect—" Mr. Crowe began.

"Jupe's solved the mystery!" Peter blurted out.

"Well," Jupiter said, "most of it, I think."

"Splendid, Jupiter!" Mr. Crowe exclaimed. "Tell me!"

"Yes, sir." Jupiter nodded. "Well, I got the logbook from the *Sea Wind,* and compared—"

A sudden knocking on the front door made him stop. It was urgent, agitated knocking. Mr. Crowe went out to open the door. He returned with the oil-company manager, Paul MacGruder. MacGruder glared up at the author.

"What did that Yamura want here?" he demanded.

"The Japanese businessman we saw at the wharf?" Mr. Crowe said, astonished. "He hasn't been here, MacGruder."

"What do you mean he hasn't been here?" Paul MacGruder said, equally astonished. "I saw him go into your yard almost half an hour ago, and he just came out and drove off!"

"I've never even met Yamura!" Mr. Crowe snapped.

"But I *saw* him!"

As the two men faced each other, Jupiter's eyes suddenly gleamed.

"Perhaps," the stout boy said, "he was only
watching the house. Spying on Mr. Crowe!"

"You mean," Bob exclaimed, "for the oil company?"

"Or for some other reason," Jupiter said. "Perhaps
he isn't here just to consult with the oil company."

There was a silence in the study. Paul MacGruder
nodded.

"He's been here over a week, and he hasn't visited
the drilling platform or the wharf until today," the
slender manager said. "Tonight I heard him talking
on the phone about Crowe and the protest, so when he
left in a hurry, I followed. He came right here."

"What could he want with me?" Mr. Crowe
wondered.

MacGruder shrugged. "There seems to be some
funny business going on," he said seriously. "Like at
the wharf today. I don't mean the arrogant way
Hanley acted—that's what I expect from him. But it
looked like some of your protesters were trying to *help*
Hanley—by deliberately starting a riot and forcing
the police to step in and perhaps ban the whole protest
action."

"That's ridiculous!" Mr. Crowe snapped.

"Maybe," Paul MacGruder said, "but something's
going on. The near riot, the sabotage on the drilling
platform, the tampering with your boat—as if
someone were trying to discredit you all."

"Gosh," Jupiter said innocently, "it sounds as if you want the protest to *win*. I mean, even if you work for the oil company."

MacGruder's face darkened as he looked at Jupiter.

"It's my job to produce oil, young man," he said, "but it's everyone's job to think of the environment. Even an oil man's."

MacGruder walked out. Soon they heard a car start out in the street and drive away. In the study, the only sound was the Coast Guard announcer reporting that the Baja hurricane was now moving north toward land and was expected to lose its force over the Baja peninsula.

"Why would Yamura spy on me?" Mr. Crowe asked.

"If he did," Bob said. "I mean, we only have MacGruder's word."

"Yes," Jupiter agreed. "But if Yamura was spying, why does Mr. MacGruder care? He acts as if he wants the protest to continue."

"Who cares about all that!" Pete cried. "Jupe, the mystery! Why is the *Sea Wind* losing that fuel?"

Jupiter grinned, and paused dramatically. "Because it's been carrying something heavy out to the platform!"

6

Jupiter Finds
an Answer

"That's impossible, Jupiter!" Mr. Crowe said.

"No, sir," Jupiter insisted. "It must be true."

"How could we carry anything out there and not know it?"

"I don't know that yet," Jupiter admitted, "but I know you *are* carrying something out, and something heavy too. That's the only possible answer to the mystery of the fuel loss."

"Are you sure, First?" Bob said dubiously.

"I'm sure," Jupiter said firmly. "Mr. Crowe and Captain Jason inspected the engine, the fuel tanks, and the fuel lines, and they found nothing out of order. They checked the fuel gauges and actually measured the tanks with a dip stick. The *Sea Wind* had full tanks for every trip to the platform. No one could have stolen any fuel at sea, and no one was seen going onto the boat while it was tied up in the marina. So——"

"But, Jupe," Bob interrupted, "if no one went onto the *Sea Wind*, how could anything have been put on the boat?"

"I don't know that yet either," Jupiter acknowledged, "but somehow it happened."

The leader of The Three Investigators looked at the others defiantly. Bob and Pete shifted uneasily in their chairs. Mr. Crowe watched Jupiter, and then nodded.

"All right, Jupiter. Go on with your explanation. We'll listen. What brought you to your conclusion?"

"The *Sea Wind*'s logbook, sir, and some simple reasoning," Jupiter explained. "First, since you had the right amount of fuel all but four times, Captain Jason's calculation of the amount of fuel needed to go out to the platform, stay all day, and come back had to be correct. Second, it seemed clear that no fuel had actually been lost through leaks, theft, or engine malfunction. Third, if no fuel had been *lost,* then that had to mean that the *Sea Wind* had simply *used* more fuel on those four days."

"Yes," Mr. Crowe nodded, "that sounds logical. But . . . ?"

"But why and how was the *Sea Wind* using more fuel on some days than others? Right, sir," Jupiter went on. "Well, the first possibility, of course, was some change in the operation of the engine. But we had already ruled that out. The second possibility was some change in the fuel itself. Perhaps it was different on the four days, maybe a lower grade that gave less mileage."

"That's a good idea, Jupe!" Pete declared.

"I thought it was, so I checked with Captain Jason when I picked up the logbook to see if he had bought fuel at a different place on those four days."

"He hadn't," Mr. Crowe said. "We thought of that too, Jupiter. But Captain Jason always bought our fuel at the same marine depot in the marina."

"Yes, he told me, and it isn't likely that the fuel at one depot would change drastically from day to day," Jupiter said. "The third possibility was that for some reason the *Sea Wind* had sailed *farther* on those four days. For some reason it had gone a longer distance. But you hadn't mentioned taking any side trips or detours, and the logbook confirmed that. I doubted that both you and Captain Jason could have overlooked or forgotten four side trips!"

"We made no detours," Mr. Crowe agreed.

"So," Jupiter continued, "you hadn't lost the fuel, the engine was operating normally, your fuel hadn't changed, and you were sailing essentially the same distance every day. As far as I could see, that left only one more possibility—*time*. Had it taken you *longer* to get out and back on those four days? I was suddenly sure that it must have, and the logbook confirmed my reasoning!"

He looked triumphantly at them. "The log showed that, on those four days that you ran short of fuel, you had arrived at the platform approximately *fifteen minutes later!* It took you fifteen minutes longer to get out to the platform on those four days, and fifteen minutes longer to get back on three of the days! In the confusion of controlling all those boats and protesters, you never noticed those fifteen minutes."

Mr. Crowe sat there dumbfounded.

"Clearly," Jupiter continued, "something slowed the *Sea Wind* down on those four days. You had already checked out the tides, currents, and winds and found nothing unusual. That left me with only one answer—on those days the *Sea Wind* must have been carrying a heavier load! The extra weight would slow it down, so it would use more fuel to go the same distance!"

Mr. Crowe suddenly laughed. "Of course! It's so obvious, isn't it? Such a simple explanation!"

"Very simple," Jupiter said drily. "Elementary."

"I'm sorry, Jupiter," Mr. Crowe said quickly. "Other people always say how simple it is *after* the detective explains his deductions, don't they? But I missed the solution completely. You've done a fine piece of reasoning. Good work!"

"Thank you, sir," Jupiter said, looking pleased. He took a sheet of yellow notepad paper from his pocket. "And since I had some time at the motel, I worked out about how much extra weight the *Sea Wind* had to be carrying. From the miles per gallon it gets, the speed, the distance, and the gallons you were short, I calculate a weight of about two thousand pounds—carried both ways, except for that first time when you got back in okay. That time you must have carried the extra weight only one way. I don't really understand why yet."

"Two thousand pounds?" Pete exclaimed.

"Gee, First," Bob wondered, "how could anything that big be hidden on the boat? How could it even get onto the boat?"

"It does seem crazy," Jupiter admitted.

"Swell!" Pete groaned. "You solve a mystery—and come right up with another! Now how do we solve that one?"

"By watching the *Sea Wind* tonight, and every night from now on, until we find the solution," Jupiter announced.

"Torao is already watching the boat, Jupiter," Mr. Crowe reminded them. "And later on Captain Jason will watch, starting at midnight."

"I know, sir," Jupiter said, "but they were watching it before. Somehow, whoever is behind this got something on board without their seeing him."

"Maybe he's invisible," Bob suggested with a smile.

"Oh no!" Pete gulped. "Not a ghost!"

Jupiter shook his head impatiently. "Be serious,

fellows! There are no ghosts. Now, what we have to do is watch the boat without being seen ourselves. Not even by Torao or Captain Jason."

"You don't mean that you think it could be one of them!" Mr. Crowe said.

"It could be anyone," Jupiter said grimly. "We not only don't know what you've been carrying or how it got aboard the *Sea Wind*, but we don't know *why* it's there!"

"All right," Mr. Crowe agreed. "I won't tell anyone what you're doing, but I have to be there with you."

Jupiter shook his head. "It's possible that you're being watched, sir. You have to stay here at your house to make sure no one suspects what we're doing. You can help us get started, but then you'll have to leave us alone."

Mr. Crowe nodded reluctantly. "When will you begin?"

"Right now," Jupiter declared. "We'll go to our motel to get some equipment and tell Bob's father where we're going. Then we'll go straight to the *Sea Wind* and search it from stem to stern to be sure nothing is on board already!"

7

Bob in Danger!

Half an hour later, with Torao and Mr. Crowe, the
Investigators had searched the whole boat and found
nothing!

"You'd better go back to your motel and get some
sleep," Mr. Crowe said to the boys. "Torao, just
watch and report anything you see. Don't try to stop
anyone who comes to the boat. Hide if you have to.
Just tell me about it later. Okay?"

"Yes, sir, very good." The Japanese youth bobbed
his head up and down vigorously. "Torao do."

"Come on, boys," Mr. Crowe said.

They got into Mr. Crowe's car and drove off. The
moment they were out of sight of the *Sea Wind*, Mr.
Crowe stopped the car in a dark and hidden corner of
the marina parking lot.

"I'll go on home and make sure I can be seen," the

author said. "Now be careful, boys. We don't know what's going on, so if there is any trouble, call me at once."

The three detectives nodded. When Mr. Crowe had driven away, the boys crouched down in the dark parking lot. They were wearing dark clothes, and were almost invisible in the night. Jupiter took three flashlights from his pockets.

"I bought these while you two were out with Bob's father," he explained. "After delivering the answer to the fuel mystery, I knew a night watch would be our next step. Now, I've covered each lens with black paper that's had a small cross, circle, or triangle cut out of it. I'll take the one with the cross, Bob can have the triangle, and Pete the circle. That way, when we separate, we can signal each other in Morse code and we'll know exactly who is giving the signal!"

"Hey, that's a great idea, First," Pete declared.

"Well," Jupiter admitted reluctantly, "it wasn't mine. I read about it. The English used this kind of signal during World War Two blackouts in London. Okay, let's take up our positions!"

The boys moved stealthily ahead to the dark and silent marina. Hundreds of boats creaked against docks, and forests of masts stood up eerily against the dark sky. Pete slipped past the *Sea Wind*, tied up to the sea wall, and out onto a wooden pier. He found a spot where he could watch the water side of the boat.

Jupiter crept down the sea wall toward the breakwater and crouched behind a row of barrels, from where he could see the whole front deck. Bob lay under the bow of a catamaran that had been hoisted up on the sea wall. He had a clear view of the rear deck of the big work boat.

In the quiet night the Investigators waited.

An hour passed.

From time to time the boys flashed their lights quickly to reassure each other that they were still in position and had seen nothing yet.

By eleven o'clock, Pete was getting restless at his post out on the pier. He could see nothing on the silent *Sea Wind*—not even the gardener, Torao, who was somewhere on the boat. He raised his flashlight to signal, and froze!

Someone had come into the marina from the harbor boulevard and was silently approaching the *Sea Wind!* A shadowy figure moving quickly but stealthily, like someone in a hurry who did not want to be seen.

The skulking figure reached the *Sea Wind,* and . . . Pete gulped. There wasn't one figure, there were two! Two dark shadows that stood close together on the sea wall, as if conferring. Pete strained to see. He could just make out the outlines of the shadowy figures. They had broad shoulders and wore heavy jackets. Both men were the same size, and seemed to have some kind of shapeless hats on their heads. Wool hats! They were the abalone divers from Oxnard who had started the trouble on the wharf! The Connors brothers!

The two men looked around, then climbed aboard the *Sea Wind*.

Jupiter's faint cross flashed in the night—a short message in Morse code: A-L-E-R-T.

Pete flashed once to show he had gotten the message, and watched the dark boat. From his position he could see the entire boat outlined against the sea wall. The shadowy shapes of the two Connors brothers appeared and disappeared as they moved around. First the men were in the bow, then at the stern, and then they disappeared entirely.

Had they gone? Pete listened intently. No, he could hear faint sounds coming from the *Sea Wind*— from somewhere below deck. What were the men up to, and where was the young Japanese gardener, Torao? The sounds of movement below decks went on for a while longer. Then the two abalone divers emerged on deck again. They climbed off the boat and turned toward the waterfront boulevard.

Bob's tiny triangle flashed in the night: I FOLLOW.

Crouched low, Pete left his post and crawled back to Jupiter's hiding place behind the barrels.

"Shouldn't we go with him, First?" he whispered.

"No," Jupiter said. "Only one person can shadow properly. More are too easily spotted." The leader of the trio peered ahead, watching Bob slip away from under the catamaran and vanish after the Connors brothers. "Besides, I want to go aboard the *Sea Wind* and see if they put anything on the boat. Maybe Torao saw where—"

Jupiter broke off abruptly, and stared in the direction the Connors brothers and Bob had gone.

"Pete!" His voice was alarmed. "There's someone else! Look, coming out of the parking lot near the place where Bob was hiding!"

Pete saw the quick shadow of a man coming from the parking lot and moving rapidly off in the same direction as Bob and the abalone divers.

"He's tailing Bob!" Pete exclaimed softly.

"Records could be in danger," Jupiter said. "I'll go after them all and warn Bob! You stay here!"

"Hurry, Jupe!" Pete urged. "I'll see if I can find Torao, and maybe spot what the Connors brothers were doing!"

Jupiter nodded quickly, and hurried off along the sea wall toward the harbor promenade. He kept to the shadows, his eyes fixed on the small figure ahead. The newcomer appeared to be watching someone ahead of him. Bob or the Connors brothers? wondered Jupe.

Back on the sea wall, Pete crouched behind the barrels and watched Jupiter and his quarry vanish into the night. After a time he became aware that no cars had started up near the marina. Wherever the

Connors brothers and the shadowy third man were going, they were on foot. That meant that Bob and Jupe could follow them without any trouble, but it also meant that the boys might not get back for a long time.

Pete was on his own. He looked hard at the dark shape of the *Sea Wind*. Had Jed and Tim Connors put something on board? If they had, had Torao spotted it? Where was Torao?

The athletic Second Investigator moved softly and rapidly across the concrete sea wall to the dark boat bobbing gently on the water. Nothing moved on the boat, and he saw no sign of the young Japanese gardener.

Pete climbed aboard the boat and crouched down.

"Torao?" he said softly.

Pete listened hard, but there was no answer.

He moved quietly along the forward deck to the bridge.

"Torao?"

Something seemed to move back near the stern. Pete stood up and peered into the darkness where the movement had caught his eye.

He heard the heavy footsteps behind him too late!

A strong hand gripped his shoulder!

"Just stand right there!"

The deep voice was harsh and threatening, and the grip held Pete like a vise.

8

A Double Chase

Bob crossed the promenade and the adjoining harbor boulevard, keeping to the darkest part of the street, and then walked close to the walls of the buildings on the other side. The two abalone divers were well in front of him. The brothers seemed to be arguing, with the one in the red hat, Tim Connors, doing most of the talking, and Jed Connors, in the black hat, listening.

The men walked on two more blocks east, still arguing and never looking back. Bob followed silently. Then the men turned north on a side street, into a neighborhood of warehouses and feed and fish stores, all dark and closed now. Partway up the street stood a large old hotel, shabby and rundown. There was little light coming from the hotel itself; dark green shades covered most of the windows. But, on the ground floor, glaring neon signs announced a tavern: Blue Shark Bar.

The Connors brothers turned into the tavern, letting a wave of violent noise and music pour out into the night. The noise and music cut off abruptly as the Blue Shark's door closed behind them.

Bob stood dismayed in the shadows of a warehouse. He had never been inside a tavern at night, and this one looked rough and gaudy. It was obviously a fishermen's and sailors' bar. Bob knew he would stand out if he went inside. But he couldn't just wait outside for the Connors brothers. He had to know what they were up to!

He looked at his dark sweater, pants, and shoes. Maybe he could pass for a fisherman's son looking for his father. He took a deep breath and crossed the street to the tavern. The noise and music blasted in his face as he opened the door.

Smoke swirled in the dim light inside a long, low room filled with crowds of rough-looking men.

"Hey you! Kid! What you up to?"

An enormously fat man in dirty corduroy pants and a greasy yachting cap blocked Bob's way.

"I—I—" Bob stammered.

"Beat it! You hear? No kids in here! Go on!".

Gulping, Bob hastily backed out and the fat man closed the door in his face. Chagrined, and angry at himself for not telling the fat man some story, Bob stared in frustration at the closed door. He couldn't get into the tavern that way now. The fat man would never listen to any story!

Bob glanced up and down the empty street. On the side of the hotel away from the harbor there was an alley. A small sign pointing into it read: Blue Shark Deliveries. Bob walked quickly to the mouth of the alley. If the Blue Shark Bar got its deliveries from the alley, then there had to be an entrance from the alley into the tavern!

The alley was narrow and dark. Bob advanced cautiously between windowless brick walls. The alley made a sharp turn at the rear of the hotel. Around the turn, rows of large garbage cans stood on either side of a door with a dim light over it.

The door was unlocked.

On the *Sea Wind,* Pete squirmed in the hard grip of the unseen man behind him.

"What are you doing on this boat, boy?" the harsh voice demanded.

"I—I—" Pete stammered, his mind racing as he tried to think of a good reason for being on the *Sea Wind* without revealing what the boys were really doing!

"Well, can't you talk, boy?" the voice snapped. "I warn you, you're in great trouble! If you don't want to face the police, you'd better explain what you're up to here!"

Suddenly Pete noticed that the shadow he had seen in the stern of the boat was moving again! It was the Japanese gardener, Torao! If the youth could get behind Pete's attacker, maybe together they could . . . Pete groaned inside—his plans were wrecked! Torao was walking straight toward him and his captor!

"Friend of Meester Crowe," Torao said, bobbing his head and smiling. "Come watch boat."

"What?" The man said behind Pete. "Put on the bridge light, Torao."

Torao switched on the light on the bridge. The man turned Pete to face him. Pete recognized the bearded Captain Jason, still wearing his heavy pea jacket and old Navy officer's cap. The captain released his grip on Pete's shoulder.

"You're one of the boys who came aboard the *Sea Wind* out at the platform. I remember now. Which one are you?"

"Pete Crenshaw, sir."

"Okay, Pete, now what's this about watching the *Sea Wind*?"

Pete hastily explained what the Investigators were doing, and what Jupiter had deduced.

"Two thousand pounds!" the bearded captain exclaimed. "That's impossible. No one could hide anything of that size on the *Sea Wind* without my knowing it."

"We know it sounds crazy, Captain Jason," Pete

agreed, "but Jupiter is sure that it's the only possible answer to your fuel loss."

Captain Jason thought awhile, then shook his head.

"I have to admit that your friend's calculations would explain the fuel loss, and I haven't been able to think of any good explanation myself. Still . . ."

"Captain," Pete said, "a little while ago we saw those two Connors brothers, Jed and Tim, come aboard the *Sea Wind*. They weren't carrying anything big, but maybe somehow they got something on board. Maybe Torao saw what it was and where it's hidden!"

"Hear men," Torao said. "Not see. Meester Crowe say hide. I hide."

"There was another man, too," Pete added. "We didn't see who it was, and he didn't come onto the boat, but he was sure hanging around and watching."

"Then we'd better search the boat right now," Captain Jason said.

As Pete followed the bearded captain below deck, he looked at his watch. It wasn't even 11:30 yet. Captain Jason wasn't supposed to start watching the *Sea Wind* until midnight. Why had he come early?

Jupiter had followed the third man across the harbor boulevard and down a side street. The man was obviously following someone ahead of him. He stopped in front of a rundown hotel. On the ground floor was a neon-lighted tavern, the Blue Shark Bar.

In the red and blue light of the neon signs, Jupiter saw the man's thin face.

It was the oil-company manager, Paul MacGruder.

MacGruder hesitated in front of the tavern door as if considering whether to enter or not. Then he walked on and turned into an alley that ran between the hotel and the next building.

Jupiter's eyes searched the street in all directions for any sign of Bob or the Connors brothers. The whole dark street was silent and empty. Jupiter hurried to the entrance to the alley and peered between the buildings.

He saw nothing. Not even Paul MacGruder.

He went into the alley. Keeping close to the wall where the shadows were darkest, Jupiter moved nervously ahead. When the alley turned behind the hotel, Jupiter got down on his hands and knees and looked cautiously around the corner. The alley ended at a high wall on the far side of the hotel. A dead end.

And there was no one in the alley.

Alarmed, Jupiter jumped up and hurried around the corner. There was nothing in the alley except rows of garbage cans. Then he saw the door at the back of the hotel. MacGruder must have gone inside. Jupiter had his hand on the doorknob when he heard the ghostly voice.

"*Jupiter . . . Jones . . . beware!*"

He whirled.

The alley was still empty!

"*Beware . . . Jupiter . . . Jones! . . . Tremble! . . .*"
The ghostly voice seemed to come from nowhere!
"I . . . I don't believe . . ." Jupiter began.
"*Believe . . . Jupiter Jones!*" the ghostly voice said.
Not ten feet from Jupiter the top of a garbage can began to rise into the air!

9

Some Suspicious Encounters

The lid of the garbage can rose higher in the dark alley. A head came slowly up out of the can! The ghostly voice whispered: "Hi, Jupe!"

A grinning face appeared, wearing the lid of the garbage can like a hat. Bob!

"Bob!" Jupiter moaned softly. He wiped the sweat off his plump face. "That wasn't funny! And somebody could have heard you!"

"Sorry, First," Bob said, "but I just couldn't resist when I saw you out there sneaking around!"

Bob grinned again in spite of himself, and now Jupiter reluctantly smiled, too. He glanced around, but no one seemed to have seen or heard them. Bob climbed out of the garbage can.

"But what were you doing in there, Records?" Jupe asked.

Bob brushed dirt from his clothes. "I followed those Connors guys to the tavern in there. Then I came back here and found the back door. I was about to sneak inside when I heard someone coming, so I jumped into the empty can to hide."

"He didn't see you?"

Bob shook his head. "No, I don't think so, but I didn't get a look at him, either. I just heard him open the door and go inside."

"It was that Paul MacGruder," Jupiter said, and explained how he and Pete had seen MacGruder go after Bob and the Connors brothers.

"You think he was *with* the other two?" Bob asked. "Maybe their lookout while they went aboard the *Sea Wind*?"

"I don't know, Records," Jupiter said. "I don't know if he was with them, or watching them for some reason, or there by himself to sneak aboard the *Sea Wind* but they got there first. I don't know if he saw you go after them or not, or if he was tailing you or them. The only way we'll find out is to go into the tavern and try to watch them all."

Bob gulped. "You're sure, Jupe? I mean, that looks like a rough place. Maybe we should get Mr. Crowe first."

"We don't have time," Jupiter said urgently. "Perhaps if we go in the back way and stay hidden we won't even be noticed. Come on."

Jupiter opened the alley door cautiously, and the two boys quickly slipped inside. They found themselves in a dark narrow corridor with storage rooms opening off each side and the sound of kitchen activity ahead. Beyond the kitchen noises they could hear the loud music and voices in the bar itself.

"We can't go through the kitchen, First," Bob whispered.

"Not without being seen," Jupiter agreed, "but perhaps we won't have to. It looks to me as if this corridor meets a cross corridor up ahead."

They inched forward, trying not to make the smallest sound. The kitchen was just on the other side of the cross corridor. To the right, the cross corridor ended at what looked like a locked door. But to the left, the cross corridor seemed to turn toward the noise of the tavern itself.

"Hurry, Records," Jupiter urged, "before someone comes out of the kitchen!"

With the kitchen noises covering them, the boys went along the cross corridor until it turned past the rest rooms. A door directly ahead opened into the tavern. They slipped through the door into the smoke, noise, and dim light of the long, low room. Right next to the door stood a long coat rack with a few jackets hanging on it. The boys quickly stepped behind the rack, and peered out at the room.

Along the right side of the tavern was a bar with

stools. The rest of the floor space was packed with tables full of loud men. Bob looked nervously around for the fat bouncer, but didn't see him. Then his eye was caught by a table halfway across the room.

"Jupe!" Bob whispered, nudging him in the ribs.

The two Connors brothers were stitting at a table with Paul MacGruder! MacGruder was talking vehemently while the other two leaned back in their chairs and listened. All three men were drinking beer.

"We've got to get closer!" Jupe whispered. "I want to hear what they're saying."

"You're crazy!" said Bob. "We can't come out in the open here! We'll get bounced out in a minute."

"That's a chance we'll have to take. It's pretty dark in here. Walk slowly, keep your head down, and stay by the walls. Maybe we won't be noticed in the crowd."

Before Bob could protest, Jupiter had left the shelter of the coat rack and was inching along the left-hand wall. Bob shuffled after him, trying to keep an eye on MacGruder and the Connors brothers. Suddenly MacGruder stood up and pushed his chair back.

"MacGruder's leaving!" Bob exclaimed in Jupe's ear.

The oil-company manager headed for the door, but then changed direction and went over to the bar. He stopped there next to a short, bald man in a dark suit.

The man looked at him, and Bob gasped.

"It's that Japanese businessman!" Bob whispered.

"Yamura. Yes," Jupiter said softly, his voice excited. "He seems awfully busy at other things besides finding oil."

"Maybe he's just sightseeing. He was all alone at the bar there."

"This isn't a tourist spot," Jupiter said. "Look! The Connors brothers seem very interested in MacGruder and him."

At their table, the two abalone divers were watching MacGruder and Yamura intently. The one in the red wool hat, Tim Connors, seemed about to get up.

"Hey! You kids! What're you doin' in here?"

The enormously fat man was suddenly in front of Jupiter. His thick body blocked their view of everything else in the room. He stared at Bob and swore violently.

"Didn't I tell you not to come in here? Okay, now you're in real trouble. I oughtta bust your head—"

A hard voice spoke behind the fat man. "They came for us, Marco. We been waiting for them."

In his red hat, Tim Connors stood beside the fat man and smiled at the boys. The fat man looked dubious.

"Kids ain't supposed to be in here, Connors," he growled.

"Sure, Marco," Tim Connors agreed. "They won't stay long. Just came to deliver a message to Jed and me. Right, boys?"

"Yes, sir," Jupiter said. "A private message."

"Right," Tim Connors said. "Come over to our table."

The fat man continued to glare at the boys, but finally shrugged.

"Okay, Connors, but you get 'em out of here fast!"

He waddled away through the smoky room, and Tim Connors led the boys to his table. Jupiter looked toward the bar.

"Bob," he whispered, "MacGruder and Yamura are gone!"

Bob could only nod before they reached the table. Jed Connors watched them closely as they sat down.

"You kids could get in bad trouble here," he said. "What're you doing, looking for Crowe? Is he around here somewhere?"

"How do you know us, Mr. Connors?" Jupiter asked.

"Same way you know us," Jed Connors said. "Saw you with Crowe down at the wharf today."

Tim Connors grinned. "Guess Crowe is kinda mad at us, huh? All that fuss at the wharf." His smile became a scowl. "But those oil people just make my blood boil!"

"Then why were you talking with one of them?"

Bob blurted out. "Why did MacGruder follow you—" He bit his lip and turned red, looking at Jupiter in dismay.

"Aha!" Jed Connors said. "So you were watching the *Sea Wind* for Crowe, eh? Well, tell you the truth, we were doing almost the same thing. We went over to the *Sea Wind* earlier tonight to talk to Cap'n Jason. He wasn't on board, but then we saw this MacGruder guy hanging around. The way someone's been sabotaging the *Sea Wind,* we got suspicious and decided to tail him."

"He led us a chase around town," Tim said, "and ended up back at the harbor over on the oil wharf. We saw him get a boat and start rowing across to the marina! We ran along the beach to keep an eye on him but lost him in the dark. But we figured out where he was going!"

Jed took up the story. "So we watched the *Sea Wind* for a while from the beach. We didn't see anything, so decided to have a look on the *Sea Wind.* We went aboard, but we didn't see anything that looked funny, so we left and came here."

"We saw you," Jupiter admitted, "and followed you here."

"Next thing we know," Tim said, "MacGruder shows up and comes right over to us. He says he's seen *us* go on the *Sea Wind,* and wants to know if we spotted anything! We didn't let on we'd been tailing him. We just told him we'd taken something on board for Crowe. Don't know if he believed us or not, but he's sure up to something."

Jupiter nodded. "What about that Mr. Yamura?"

"Who?" Tim said.

"Hey," Jed said, "he must mean that Japanese guy that MacGruder was talking to! The old guy at the wharf with Hanley. Maybe he's up to some tricks for the oil company, too!"

"Wouldn't surprise me," Tim said. "All these oil guys hang together no matter what country they come from."

"Yeah." Jed nodded, and glanced behind him. "You kids better get out of here now. Tell Crowe what we saw, okay?"

"We will," Jupiter said. "Come on, Bob."

They walked through the smoke and noise and out into the street. Jupiter turned toward the harbor.

"You believe that story, First?" Bob asked.

"I don't know," Jupiter mused. "It could be true—MacGruder has been acting strange. But maybe we can find out for sure. Come on."

They hurried toward the marina.

10

Pete Comes Through

Captain Jason shook his head. "There's nothing on this boat, light or heavy, that isn't supposed to be here!"

The bearded master of the *Sea Wind* had just finished a complete search of his vessel. Now he leaned on the forward rail while Pete sat on a low hatch. Torao stood looking at both of them with the eager face of someone who doesn't understand what is being said.

"What's more," Captain Jason added, "there isn't any place on this boat where anything that large could be hidden!"

"Everything sure is clear and empty below decks," Pete admitted unhappily. "But I know Jupe's got to be . . ." He stopped ahd listened. "Someone's coming!"

"Down!" Captain Jason whispered.

They listened in the night, but there was no sound now. They waited, barely breathing. Nothing happened.

Then two faint points of light split the night. A tiny cross and a tiny triangle!

"It's Bob and Jupe!" Pete exclaimed. "They must have been alarmed when they saw people on the boat. They won't come close until they know who we are."

He flashed his small circle in return, and soon Jupiter and Bob appeared on the sea wall. They climbed aboard.

"Why are you on the boat with the lights on, Second?" Jupiter demanded. "Someone else might come to—"

"Captain Jason thought I was a trespasser," Pete explained, "and then he wanted to search the boat up and down. With all the commotion and light, I figured we'd blown our cover anyway."

Captain Jason added, "No one told me you were watching the *Sea Wind* and that everyone was supposed to keep out of sight. I came down here early to relieve Torao. When I heard from Pete that someone might have put something on my boat, I wanted to know what!"

"Yes, sir, I see." Jupiter nodded thoughtfully. "Did you find—"

"More come!" Torao said suddenly.

Footsteps were coming along the sea wall from the direction of the harbor promenade. Someone was in a hurry. The group on board waited. Finally Mr. Crowe appeared in the light of the *Sea Wind*. He came aboard looking anxious.

"Is everything all right? You're all safe? Torao, too?"

"Of course, sir," Jupiter said. "But I thought you were going to remain at your house."

"I know," Mr. Crowe said, "but Torao was supposed to report before he went home at midnight. It's almost one A.M., and he hasn't reported. I got worried."

The Investigators described everything that had happened since the time Crowe left them. Captain Jason added a word about searching the boat.

"You found nothing?" Mr. Crowe asked.

"Not a thing," Captain Jason growled.

"And MacGruder followed the Connors brothers, and then joined them in that bar?"

"Yes, sir." Bob nodded. "That Mr. Yamura was there too."

"Do you believe the Connors brothers' story?" Crowe asked.

"I'm not sure," Jupiter answered. He turned to the young Japanese gardener. "Torao, did anyone else come on board the *Sea Wind*? From the *water* side, and *before* the Connors brothers arrived?"

Torao tried to find words. "Two men, same time. Not see other. Hide. Not see good. Sorry."

"Jupe?" Pete said. "I was watching the water side. I'd have seen a boat row up, and I didn't see anything."

"Then they're lying!" Mr. Crowe fumed. "I'll bet they're the ones who are lousing up the *Sea Wind!*"

"Not necessarily," Jupiter said, frowning. "Torao might have missed someone who was being very cautious. MacGruder could have left his boat somewhere and *swum* up to the *Sea Wind*. Maybe he climbed aboard from the water, and Pete never spotted him."

"MacGruder's a scuba diver, too," Mr. Crowe exclaimed. "He could have been wearing a wetsuit under his clothes. In the dark, Pete could easily have missed a man in a black wetsuit!"

"I guess I could have," Pete admitted.

"But," Bob pointed out, "no one put anything on the boat tonight. So the Connors brothers could be telling the truth about MacGruder being in a rowboat, and MacGruder could still be doing nothing to the *Sea Wind*."

"Yes, I suppose so," Jupiter agreed, dejected.

"And we still don't know how anything so big and heavy could be hidden on the boat," Mr. Crowe said. "Well, it's getting very late. I think we should all call it a night. You, too, Captain. There doesn't seem to be any point to guarding the boat all night. If someone puts a heavy object on board before morning, we'll spot it easily enough. Why don't you drive Torao to his rooming house, Captain, and I'll take the boys to their motel."

Captain Jason nodded and left the boat with Torao. The Investigators waited in the bow while Mr. Crowe went to turn off the bridge light and lock up. Pete stood at the railing, staring down into the dark water.

"We can sleep on it, boys," the author said when he returned. "Tomorrow—"

Pete turned at the railing, his eyes suddenly wide.

"Maybe it isn't *on* the boat," he said excitedly. "Maybe it's *under* the boat!"

The others stared at the tall Second Investigator.

"I mean," he exclaimed, "Captain Jason says there's no place on the boat that anything so big could be hidden. But it could be *on* the boat without being *in* the boat—attached underneath!"

"And," Bob added, "the Connors brothers and MacGruder are all scuba divers! Any of them could have attached the weight!"

Jupiter cried, "Pete! I think you've hit on it!"

"Underneath it wouldn't even have to be very big to slow the boat down!" Pete went on. "There'd be a heavy drag!"

"Gosh, maybe just a diver himself is hanging on?" Bob suggested.

Pete shook his head. "Too small, Bob. Anyway, a diver couldn't hang on at the *Sea Wind*'s top speed. Even if he was hooked on, his mask and tank would get torn off."

"But what would anyone want to attach to the boat?" Mr. Crowe wondered. "And why?"

"Some kind of listening device?" Bob said. "So the oil-company people could hear everything you said?"

"Not big enough, Records," Pete said. "Maybe a big camera or something?"

"Why, Pete?" Mr. Crowe asked. "All we do is go out to the platform, sail around protesting, and come back."

Jupiter suddenly broke in. "Unless someone was taking something out to the platform, or bringing something in! Something secret. Something that needed a large container! They sent the container out to the platform under the *Sea Wind,* divers from the platform put whatever it was into the container underwater, and the *Sea Wind* brought it to shore unseen! Something illegal!"

"Smuggling!" Bob and Pete cried.

Jupiter nodded. "Someone brings whatever it is to the oil platform from somewhere abroad, and then uses the *Sea Wind* to smuggle it ashore!"

"But why me?" demanded Mr. Crowe. "Why use *my* boat?"

"Because you're the protest leader. You go out to

the platform every day without fail," Jupe pointed out. "That's why the smuggler had to look at the schedule in your notebook, sir—so he would know when you were going out and coming back in!"

Mr. Crowe was stunned. "And the police would never think of searching under our protest boats!"

"A perfect setup for a smuggler!" Bob exclaimed.

Mr. Crowe nodded. "That first time when we ran low on fuel but didn't actually run out—maybe that was a test run! They sent the container out to be sure it would work, and then just took it away."

"MacGruder's beginning to look like a logical suspect," Jupiter said slowly. "He has easy access to the platform. He hasn't been against the protest, and he hasn't wanted the police to break it up, even though he's an oil man. Smuggling would explain his behavior."

"Maybe that Mr. Yamura is some kind of policeman," Pete suggested, "and that's why MacGruder is worried about him."

"Then," Mr. Crowe said, "let's find MacGruder first thing in the morning!"

"No," Jupiter said. "We don't have any real proof yet. But I think we can find our first evidence tonight!"

"Gosh, Jupe, how?" Pete wondered.

"By looking under the boat! Perhaps Pete didn't see MacGruder tonight because the man was underwater,

attaching a container to the hull of the *Sea Wind!* Mr.
Crowe, do you have diving equipment aboard?"

"No, Jupiter, but I do at home! I'll get it!"

"Take Pete with you, sir. He's had a full course in
scuba diving. Make sure the equipment fits him."

Mr. Crowe nodded, and hurried off to his car with
Pete.

On the *Sea Wind,* Jupiter and Bob waited. The
dark night grew colder. The boats in the marina
creaked in their berths, and the shadows seemed to
move menacingly all around. The two boys jumped at
every faint noise.

Their teeth were chattering from cold and nervous-
ness by the time Mr. Crowe and Pete returned. Pete,
excited and already in a wetsuit, didn't seem to notice
the chill. He strapped on the air tank and fitted the
breathing tube into his mouth. Sitting backward on
the outboard railing, he gave a grin and a wave and
tumbled off into the water. He fell like a stone, and
soon his underwater light could be seen moving
beneath the *Sea Wind.*

On deck, Bob, Jupiter, and Mr. Crowe waited
impatiently. From time to time they could see the
faint glow of Pete's light moving from bow to stern.
Then the light rose directly toward them, and Pete
broke the surface. He climbed aboard with their help,
and sat down on a hatch. He took off his diving mask.

"Nothing," he said. "No container, no hooks,

nothing on the boat, and no sign there ever has been anything! It's a metal hull, Jupe. There's no place to even put in a hook!"

Jupiter chewed his lip. "All right, Second. Perhaps we're wrong about MacGruder, but I'm convinced that we're on the right track. We'll go home, get some sleep, and tomorrow set a little trap!"

11

The Hitchhiker

Sudden sunlight flooded the motel room the next morning. Pete burrowed under his pillow and groaned. Jupiter flopped over onto his face like a baby whale. Bob cried, "Close those shades!"

Mr. Andrews chuckled. "Up and at 'em, boys. You left a note to wake you at seven A.M. Time to get going!"

With a cheerful laugh, Mr. Andrews left the room. The three boys lay in their beds without moving.

"I," Pete said, "hate grownups."

"No," Bob said, "just parents."

"Just parents who are cheerful at seven A.M." Jupiter added.

"An excellent point, First," Bob said.

"Agreed," Pete said. "But—I hate to admit it—we *did* leave that note."

"We must have been out of our skulls," Bob said.

Laughing, the boys leaped out of their beds. They dressed quickly in their heavy sailing clothes, and ten minutes later were digging into a huge breakfast in the motel coffee shop. Still sleepy from their late night, the boys revived as they discussed their case with Mr. Andrews.

"Smugglers, eh?" Mr. Andrews said. "Yes, it sounds like the solution, but be careful what you do, all right?"

"Mr. Crowe and Captain Jason will be with us," Pete assured him.

"Good," Mr. Andrews said, "but I'm afraid that Bob won't be. I need him for a few hours this morning."

"Gee, Dad, do I have to?" Bob protested.

"I have an important interview at the university with the leading neutral expert on oil and the environment. Meanwhile I need to get the tapes from yesterday's interviews transcribed. They can't wait. You're a good typist, Bob, so it shouldn't take you long."

"Sure, Dad. I guess the fellows can manage awhile without me."

"Gosh," Pete said, "you really think we can, Records?"

Bob threw a spoon at him and, laughing, they all finished breakfast. Mr. Andrews drove off to his interview, leaving Bob in his room listening to a tape cassette and pounding away at a portable typewriter.

Pete and Jupiter walked to Mr. Crowe's house. The author was waiting for them. As he drove the boys to the marina, he pointed out the wisps of cirrus clouds in the sky.

"I'll bet those clouds are the outer fringe of that hurricane off Mexico," he declared. "The morning weather report said the storm is still moving north. It hasn't made landfall yet on Baja the way it was supposed to do. Hurricanes almost never come near Santa Barbara, but we'll double-check with the Coast Guard before we go out."

At the marina, Mr. Crowe and Captain Jason went off to consult with the protest committee and the boat captains who were going out. The boys could hear Tim and Jed Connors loudly discussing their plans with the other sailors.

"What are we going to do, Jupe?" Pete asked.

"First, we go below out of sight," Jupiter said, leading the way down into the *Sea Wind*'s cabin. Once below, he pointed to the scuba gear. "Get dressed for diving, Pete, and stay down here under cover. But be ready to come up on deck and dive at once, okay?"

"Okay," Pete agreed, and began to put on the wetsuit.

Jupiter returned to the deck, and stood innocently watching the protesters making their plans onshore.

Fifteen minutes later Mr. Crowe returned to the boat with Captain Jason.

"The Coast Guard doesn't think the hurricane will come up this far, or come close enough to be any danger. Even if it does, it can't get here before tomorrow, so we're going out. We must keep the protest up every day. Where's Pete?"

"Down below, ready to dive," Jupiter said in a low voice. "My plan is that we'll start out exactly as you always do. But halfway across the harbor, we'll stop and Pete will dive at once! If anything is under the boat, he'll spot it."

"Good," Mr. Crowe agreed. "That should do the trick."

Mr. Crowe went to help Captain Jason get the *Sea Wind* under way. Some of the protest boats, their signs and banners up, were already on their way out of the harbor. Among them, Jupiter saw, was the black fishing boat with the flying bridge. Tim Connors was at the wheel in his red wool hat. Each boat slowed almost to a stop at the harbor sand bar, then gathered speed as it met the swell of the open channel and headed out for the islands.

"Okay, Jupiter," Mr. Crowe said from the bridge. "We're going out."

Jupiter nodded. He moved near the companionway to the cabin where Pete was hidden. The *Sea Wind* moved slowly away from the sea wall, out of the confines of the marina, and across the open harbor. When they were halfway toward the sand bar, Mr. Crowe spoke quickly to Captain Jason. The *Sea Wind* slowed. Jupiter called down the companionway.

"Okay, Pete! Now!"

As the boat came to a complete stop, Pete burst out of the companionway, rushed to the railing, turned, and fell backward over the side. Jupiter watched his underwater light vanish beneath the boat. Mr. Crowe came to join him, and Captain Jason watched from the bridge. Minutes passed slowly. Then a voice called from the other side of the boat! Pete was there in the water with his mask off.

"Nothing," he called up. "Nothing at all, First."

Jupiter looked thunderstruck. "I . . . I was . . . sure."

"Come aboard, Pete," Mr. Crowe said quietly.

Pete clambered back aboard with the help of Mr. Crowe.

"You boys want to continue on out with us?" Mr. Crowe asked.

"Jupe?" Pete said.

"I guess we were wrong," the stout leader said unhappily. "No one has been attaching anything to the hull of the boat."

"Maybe he spotted us," Pete said. "Or maybe the container just isn't going out today. Maybe tomorrow we'll—"

"Unless"—Jupiter's face brightened—"the smuggler works in two trips! He sends the container out on one trip, loads it *on* the platform, and brings it in on the next trip! So that first time wasn't a dry run—there just wasn't a container ready to bring back! And this time one isn't going out—because it's the last return trip!"

"Then let's go out!" Pete exclaimed.

Mr. Crowe nodded, and started back to the bridge. A voice called from the marina. "*Sea Wind!* Hello! John Crowe!"

The police captain, Max Berg, stood on a dock. He was waving to the boat. "Crowe, we're holding a meeting on that trouble at the wharf yesterday! The mayor wants you there!"

Mr. Crowe yelled back, "Is Hanley going to be there?"

"He is!"

"All right then!" Mr. Crowe nodded to Captain Jason. "Take me back, Captain." He turned to the boys. "The boat will still go out—we have to keep up the pressure. You can be my representatives, okay? You'll be all right with Captain Jason."

The *Sea Wind* returned to its berth to let Mr. Crowe jump off and join Captain Berg, then swung back out into the harbor. Mr. Crowe called out from shore, "When I'm finished with the meeting, I'll go home and keep in touch over the radio!"

The *Sea Wind* glided on across the harbor, slowing down almost to a full stop behind two other protest boats that were moving slowly through the narrow channel in the sand bar. When the others had cleared, Captain Jason took the *Sea Wind* slowly across the bar and out into the sparkling water of the Santa Barbara Channel.

At full speed, the long work boat surged up a high bow wave, sending spray across the deck. The swell was longer and heavier than the day before, and the *Sea Wind* tossed and rolled. Jupiter held tightly to the forward rail, looking a little green.

"It's . . . rougher today," he gulped.

"The hurricane down south," Captain Jason said from the bridge. "Its winds make waves that outrun the storm. But this swell won't slow us down much."

"What do we do when we get out there, First?" Pete asked. "I mean, we can't go under and watch the bottom of the boat all day."

Jupiter thought a moment, "We could make spot checks, or we could go below and listen. If the container is as big as I think, the smuggler should make noise under the boat when he . . ."

"Boys," Captain Jason said from the bridge, "the Connors boat is up ahead about two miles. It's the fastest after the *Sea Wind,* and we should be gaining on it. We're not!"

"You mean," Jupiter cried, "we're being slowed down!"

The captain nodded. "I'd never have noticed if it hadn't been on my mind, but we're down a couple of knots, and it's not because of wind or current. We've got extra weight aboard!"

"But there was nothing under the boat!" Pete protested.

"The sand bar!" Jupiter exclaimed. "We almost came to a full stop. Something must have been attached to us then!"

"Gosh, Jupe," Pete said, "we went slow, but we didn't really stop. No one could push anything that heavy under a moving boat."

Jupiter pulled on his lower lip. "No, but . . . something could move under us! Whatever is under there must be something that moves by itself!"

"What could move underwater except a diver?" Pete asked. "And no diver could hang on or even survive under us."

"I don't know," Jupiter admitted.

Captain Jason said, "I don't know either, but Jupiter is right. Whatever is under there can move on its own. We don't have some container riding under us, boys. We've got a hitchhiker!"

12

The Shark Hunter

Pete gulped. "What—what kind of hitchhiker?"

"A heavy one," Captain Jason said ominously.

"Something," Jupiter said, "that can hold on to a steel boat going almost twenty-five knots in a strong sea and not be hurt."

The *Sea Wind* plunged on through the heavy, sweeping swell of the channel. In silence the three people on board looked down at the deck, as if they wished they could see through the steel. Or perhaps they were just as glad that they couldn't!

"We'd better take a look, boys," Captain Jason said. "We should know what it is down there."

"I don't think I want to know!" Pete said.

"Nonsense!" said Jupiter firmly. "You're not going to find a sea monster or anything like that. Even if there were sea monsters, they wouldn't attach themselves to a boat, ride out to an oil platform, and ride back in again! No, whatever is under us is man-made. Some kind of vehicle, is my guess."

"We'll soon find out," Captain Jason said. "Pete, get—"

"Wait!" Jupiter interrupted. "What if there's a person down there? If we stop out here, whoever it is might become alarmed and drop off. We'd lose him, and maybe warn him that he had been spotted."

"Then what do we do, First?" Pete wondered.

"We had better continue on out normally. Once we're out by the platform, Pete can go over the side again and surprise whatever it is."

"You're right, Jupiter," Captain Jason agreed. "But you'd better watch port and starboard in case it drops off early."

"I'll take port!" Pete said, going to the left rail.

Jupiter took the right rail, and both boys stared down at the surging dark green water. The *Sea Wind* soon passed between Anacapa and Santa Cruz islands and turned west. The platform of Shark Reef #1 was straight ahead. Long waves rose high against its steel legs.

"Boys, I don't trust the weather," Captain Jason said suddenly from the bridge. He was staring up at the sky, which was now covered with a thin film of cloud. "That's cirrostratus cloud, and it's getting thicker. The swell is higher and faster than it should be, the barometer is unsteady, and the wind is changing direction and getting stronger. I don't like it."

"The hurricane, sir?" Jupiter said.

The captain nodded. "From all those signs, it's closer than it should be. It could be heading straight for Santa Barbara. I'd better radio the Coast Guard."

"We're almost at the platform, Captain!" Pete called.

The great steel structure towered out of the sea in the now watery sunlight. To one side, the flotilla of protest boats waited to form their circle. High above them, jeering oil-rig workers lined the railings of the platform.

Pete slipped on his air tank and mask, and Captain Jason slowed the *Sea Wind* in the heavy swell. The bearded captain watched the sea and sky anxiously as the boat moved slower.

"It's getting rough for diving," he said. "I—"

At that instant the *Sea Wind* seemed to surge ahead.

"Jupe! Captain!" Pete cried. "There it goes!"

They all looked down at the water on the port side, which faced the platform. A long, thin, torpedolike shadow shimmered beneath the surface and faded into the depths.

"It's . . . it looked like . . . a shark!" Pete exclaimed.

"No," Captain Jason said, staring down. "Not a

shark, Pete, a *Shark Hunter!* It must have hooked onto us magnetically!"

"What is a Shark Hunter, sir?" Jupiter said.

"An underwater vehicle that divers use, Jupiter. It's 'wet'—there's no air inside like in a sub, and the diver has to use his own air tanks to breathe. The Shark Hunter's about six feet long, four feet high, and three feet wide. It's electric-powered, and can carry tools and extra tanks of air."

"Or something someone is smuggling!" Jupiter said.

"So there's our hitchhiker," the captain said.

"And he's gone!" added Pete.

When his interview was over, Mr. Andrews drove back to the motel. Bob had just finished transcribing yesterday's tapes.

"Thanks, Bob. You've saved me a lot of time," said Mr. Andrews. "Now I have to go down to L.A. and file the first part of the story. Do you want to stay here? I'll be back tomorrow."

"Yes, Dad. I'll wait for Jupe and Pete."

After Mr. Andrews had gone, Bob decided to walk over to Mr. Crowe's house. He wanted to see if he could operate the ship-to-shore radio and get in touch with the *Sea Wind.* He didn't think Mr. Crowe would mind. As he walked along the east-side streets he noticed that a cloud cover had dimmed the sun and made its light a sickly yellow. A strong breeze was blowing now, swirling leaves and dust everywhere.

At the house he saw Mr. Crowe's car! Alarmed, he ran to the door and knocked. Mr. Crowe himself opened the door.

"Gosh, sir, what are you doing here?"

"Come into the study, Bob," Mr. Crowe said.

As they went back to the cluttered study, the author explained about his meeting with the police and the mayor.

"So Captain Jason and the boys went out without me," he went on. "I just got home. I've been listening to the Coast Guard. The hurricane has speeded up and changed direction. It's moving straight toward Santa Barbara and the offshore islands!"

"Gee, that sounds dangerous!"

"It isn't yet, but it will be by tonight! The storm is still several hundred miles south of us. You see, Bob, even though the winds in a hurricane are very high—seventy-five miles an hour or more—the storm itself travels rather slowly—maybe only ten or twenty miles an hour. Hurricane winds move in a huge circle around a calm center. The closer you get to the center, the fiercer the winds. Now, that whole big circle off Mexico is moving slowly toward us, and we're going to feel stronger and stronger winds as the day goes on."

"Will the center actually pass over us?"

"It's too soon to tell. The center is only about ten miles across—but the whole storm can be three hundred miles across! The center might pass us far to the west, out at sea, and we'd still get a big storm. If we're within twenty-five miles of the center we'll get a terrible storm!"

"I'd hate to be on that oil platform tonight!" said Bob with a shudder.

Mr. Crowe nodded. "Let's call the *Sea Wind,* and see how they're doing out there."

He turned to the radio. As he did, the speaker crackled. "*Sea Wind* calling John Crowe. Come in, Crowe. *Sea Wind* . . ."

On the long work boat, sailing with the other vessels in a circle around the platform, Captain Jason bent to the microphone.

"*Sea Wind* calling John Crowe. Come in, Crowe."

The radio whined in the rising wind. "Crowe here, *Sea Wind.* Is that you, Jason?"

"Affirmative. Hold on, Jupiter wants to talk to you."

On the rolling boat Jupiter took the microphone. "We've seen it, sir! It hooked on when we slowed at the sand bar—a kind of one-man submarine that needs a scuba diver to operate it. It's electric-powered, but Captain Jason says it can go only four knots, so that's why it hitched onto the *Sea Wind* to get out here! It must attach itself with some kind of strong magnet."

"Good work, Jupiter! Did you see the diver?"

"No, sir, just his vehicle. But I'm sure he doesn't know that, so he'll come back for his ride in! We'll catch him then. Right now we're watching the landing stage under the platform, in case he comes to the surface there. But it's hard to tell with all these waves."

Crowe said, "The hurricane is coming northwest toward us, and fast! How is it out there, Captain Jason?"

The captain eyed the heaving sea. "Not too bad yet. Some smaller boats have gone in, but most are still here."

"How long can you stay out?"

Jupiter gripped the microphone. "We've got to stay out all day! If we don't, we'll lose the hitchhiker, sir! Most of the boats are still here. The Connors brothers are right behind us, and they're not having any trouble. We must stay out!"

In his study, Mr. Crowe heard the open window rattle, and saw that the dark yellow light outside was fading to gray as thicker clouds covered the sun. But there was no rain yet.

"All right, Jupiter. But when the captain says it's time, you come in!"

Captain Jason came back on. "We'll be careful. If it gets really bad, we'll duck around Santa Cruz and find shelter."

"All right then, catch that hitchhiker!"

The radio went silent. Mr. Crowe sat back in his chair.

"Jason's a good sailor," he said to Bob, "and the *Sea Wind* is built for dirty weather. They'll be okay as—"

"Sir!" Bob whispered. "At the window!"

Mr. Crowe whirled. The window was empty. Bob jumped up and ran out into the hall to the back door. He flung it open and searched the yard outside with his eyes. Gusts of wind tossed the branches in the orchard. There was no one there.

"I know I saw someone! A face at the window. He must have heard everything we said! About spotting the hitchhiker and staying out until he comes back to the boat!"

Mr. Crowe looked at the empty yard. "You realize what that means, Bob? Whatever is going on, the diver out there isn't working alone!"

"So the diver doesn't have to be anyone we've been watching."

"But any of those people could still be involved with him."

"Except the Connors brothers," Bob pointed out.

"If *both* of them are out in their boat," Mr. Crowe said, "then I'd say they're not involved. But we only saw Tim when the boat went out."

Bob nodded slowly, and they both returned to Mr. Crowe's study. They sat in silence, listening to the rising force of the wind.

13

A Deadly Danger

Around Shark Reef #1, the protest boats had to battle harder and harder to keep in their circle. The sky was getting dark as thicker, lower clouds moved in. The waves pounded higher and higher up the steel legs of the drilling platform. One by one, the smaller boats gave up and headed for the shelter of the channel and the distant safety of Santa Barbara.

Pete, Jupe, and Captain Jason stood braced inside the bridge house on the plunging *Sea Wind*. Jupe was beginning to feel seasick, but he was too excited about catching the hitchhiker to pay attention to his stomach's distress.

"Barometer's down to twenty-nine point seven," Captain Jason said, as he held fast to the wheel to keep the *Sea Wind* on its course around the platform. "And this is only the outer edge of the storm!"

The first rain came in a sudden squall just after two o'clock in the afternoon. It began to fall steadily against the windows of the bridge house.

"We'll have to go in pretty soon," Captain Jason said.

High on the platform, more than forty feet above the water, the few oil workers still at the rail were no longer jeering. They watched the remaining boats and the darkening sky in silence.

"Perhaps the diver will come back early," Jupiter said hopefully. "If we're right, and his Shark Hunter attaches magnetically, we're his only way back to shore. The other boats are all wood or fiberglass."

"Maybe he's underwater and doesn't know how bad the storm is," Pete said.

"He might not, in very deep water," the captain said, "but it's only about eighty feet deep here, and less over Shark Reef." He pointed to where the water was white a half-mile or so in toward Santa Cruz Island. "He knows about the storm, all right. But he might take shelter ashore on Santa Cruz."

"If he's smuggling from the platform," Pete added, "I'll bet he's on it safe and dry right now and doesn't have to go back to shore!"

"No," Jupiter said stubbornly. "I know he'll return, and if we go in too soon we'll lose him for good!"

An hour later the rain was coming in sheets from a

low, completely black sky, the waves were breaking over the *Sea Wind*'s bow, and only four boats were left. Too few to form a circle, they sailed close together with the black Connors boat right behind the *Sea Wind*. In his red wool hat and a yellow slicker, Tim Connors stood sturdily on his open flying bridge looking like an ancient Viking. As the two boats moved as slowly as possible in the heavy seas, Connors maneuvered the black boat close to the *Sea Wind* and shouted across the short distance.

"Nice little blow, Jason!"

"It'll do!" Captain Jason shouted back.

"Going in soon?"

"Soon!"

Tim Connors laughed through the rain. "Fifty bucks we outlast you!"

"You're crazy, Connors! And keep farther off!"

Tim Connors grinned on his open bridge, and continued to sail dangerously close. The slow-moving boats were all on the seaward side of Shark Reef #1, half-turned into the wind. They were moving just fast enough to hold their distance from the platform and resist the waves' efforts to push them into the giant legs and the steel landing stage between them.

Two more boats blew their horns and turned toward the safety of the channel, leaving only the black Connors boat and the *Sea Wind*. Jupiter continued to search the dark sea desperately for any sign of the small underwater vehicle.

"Give up, Jupe!" Pete said. "You couldn't see him in this light anyway. He might even be under us already!"

"Just a little while longer!" Jupiter pleaded.

Suddenly, the Connors boat pulled away, and Tim Connors shouted back to them.

"You win, Jason! Have fun, all of you!"

With a final laugh, Connors put the black boat's engine into high gear. It quickly plunged past the platform and vanished into the rain.

"It's no use, Jupiter," Captain Jason said. "We're going in. The barometer's down another point and the wind is getting stronger all the time. If we stay out here much longer, we'll be in real danger."

Jupiter nodded sadly. "I guess so, sir."

Captain Jason put the engine into high speed. The *Sea Wind* surged ahead—and suddenly began to shake all over! A violent hammering noise came from under the stern!

"What is it?" Pete cried.

"We've hit something!" Jupiter shouted in alarm.

Captain Jason hung on to the wheel. "No! Something's broken underneath! Something's wrong with the propeller! It's twisting the shaft! If the shaft breaks, it could rip us open and sink us!"

The bearded captain cut the engine, and the *Sea Wind* wallowed helplessly in the surging sea. Captain

Jason looked over at the towering oil platform—the *Sea Wind* was drifting rapidly straight toward the steel legs!

"What do we do now?" Pete cried.

"If we speed up we could rip her open! If we don't, we'll be pushed against the platform or capsized! We've got to have power in this sea or we'll go broadside and turn over!" The captain gritted his teeth. "We've got one chance, boys! If we can just get a little power without breaking the propeller shaft. Hang on!"

The captain began to slowly raise the speed of the engine as the oil platform loomed directly ahead through the dark rain.

In his study, Mr. Crowe paced back and forth and looked out the window at the now heavy rain pouring down in his backyard. Bob sat at the window and watched the storm, too. The low black sky made it seem like dusk, even though sunset was hours away.

"It . . . it doesn't look too bad," Bob said uneasily. "I mean, I've seen a lot of storms like this."

"We're only on the edge of the hurricane, Bob," Mr. Crowe said. "But out at the islands . . . I'm going to call them! They must come in now!"

He sat down at the marine radio. "Calling the *Sea Wind*. Come in, *Sea Wind!* Captain Jason?"

He waited. Bob stood up and came over to the

radio. There was no answer. Mr. Crowe bent closer to the microphone. "*Sea Wind,* come in! Hello, Captain Jason! Come in, *Sea Wind!*"

Bob swallowed. "They . . . they've always answered before!"

"We'll wait a few minutes. Maybe they're busy."

They waited five minutes in the cluttered study as the wind and rain blew outside.

"Hello, *Sea Wind!*" Mr. Crowe said urgently into the radio. "Captain Jason! Jupiter! Pete!"

There was only silence.

"I'm going to call the Coast Guard," Mr. Crowe said. He flicked some switches. "Santa Barbara Coast Guard Station! John Crowe calling Santa Barbara Coast Guard!"

The speaker crackled. "Lieutenant Jameson here, Crowe."

"I'm unable to contact the *Sea Wind.* Are you in contact?"

"Negative. There's electrical disturbance out there. Will try to raise them."

The speaker went dead.

Minutes passed as Mr. Crowe tapped his fingers and Bob chewed a fingernail.

Finally the speaker hummed. "No response, Crowe. You're sure they're still out? All your other boats are accounted for and on the way in."

"I'm not sure of anything, Lieutenant!" Mr. Crowe

said," "but they should have called me if they were coming in!"

The lieutenant's voice was reassuring but not convincing. "It's probably just trouble with their radio, they—wait, I'm getting a transmission!"

The radio silence stretched agonizingly in the study as the rain fell harder and the wind lashed the windows. The lieutenant's voice returned.

"That was Shark Reef One, Crowe. *Sea Wind* had problems, but your people are safe on the platform! Sounded like they're in some kind of trouble with the oil people, though. Something about sabotage!"

14

A Monster
from the Sea

Paul MacGruder stood in the dim corridor of the drilling platform's lower deck. Three oil-rig workers stood behind him. The slender oil-company manager held a pistol. It was aimed straight at Pete and Jupiter, who had just climbed up the metal steps from the landing stage.

"So we've caught you red-handed!" MacGruder said angrily. "Mr. Hanley was right! You protesters *have* been sneaking on the platform and sabotaging it!"

"We're not sabotaging anything!" Pete cried hotly. "We never—"

"You were warned about trespassing!" MacGruder interrupted harshly. "Why would you try to come aboard secretly unless you were up to some mischief!"

Jupiter spoke quietly. "We had to come on the platform, sir. The *Sea Wind* was in trouble. Something went wrong with the propeller, and the shaft was shaking so badly it could have broken any moment. Captain Jason decided that our only chance was to let the boat drift close to the platform, and then risk the engine long enough to maneuver under the platform to your landing stage."

MacGruder snorted. "Maneuvering a disabled boat the size of the *Sea Wind* under the platform in this weather? You expect me to believe a yarn like that?"

"We're not liars!" Pete cried, getting madder.

"Captain Jason performed a great job of seamanship," Jupiter continued evenly. "We really had no choice, sir."

"And just where is Captain Jason now?" MacGruder demanded.

"Still down on the *Sea Wind*," Jupiter said. "He's tying it securely to the landing stage to ride out the storm."

MacGruder watched them narrowly. Then he motioned to two of the oil-rig workers to go downstairs to the landing stage.

"If your story doesn't check out," he said slowly, "I'm going to lock you all up until the storm passes and we can get to the bottom of this."

Pete was furious. "Maybe you just want us out of the way so you can do your smuggling!"

"Smuggling!" MacGruder reddened. "What are you talking about?"

"Sir," Jupiter said, "your office is onshore, isn't it? May I ask why you came out here today?"

"What business is that of yours, young man?"

"Well," Jupiter went on, "that depends on how you got out here. I guess everyone here saw you arrive?"

Jupiter smiled innocently. MacGruder looked at him closely.

"If it matters, I came out early this morning on a supply boat." He studied Jupiter. "What is this about smuggling?"

Jupiter said, "We believe someone is bringing something to the platform, and smuggling it ashore on the *Sea Wind*."

"That's ridiculous!" MacGruder snapped.

"No, sir." Jupiter shook his head. "The *Sea Wind* has recently been running short of fuel at times. We have been able to solve the mystery of why it happened." He told the oil-company manager what they had deduced and how they had discovered what was riding under the *Sea Wind*.

"You saw this one-man 'wet' submarine," Mac-Gruder said, "and you think *I* was in it? What makes you think that?"

Pete blurted out, "You've been following people, snooping around Mr. Crowe, and hanging around the *Sea Wind!* We saw you talking to the Connors brothers and Mr. Yamura in that tavern! And you sure

act like you want the protest sail to keep going even
though you work for the oil company!"

"I see," MacGruder said.

Before he could say more, the two oil-rig workers
came up from the landing stage, drenched with spray.
Captain Jason was with them, wearing a slicker. The
workers told MacGruder that the *Sea Wind* was indeed
disabled. They had heard the propeller shaft banging
when the captain had speeded the engine briefly to
position a line. MacGruder put down his gun, and
turned to Pete and Jupiter.

"I'm sorry, boys. I guess I was wrong about you.
It's just that I've been concerned about something
going on here. I wasn't in that Shark Hunter you
spotted. These men can tell you when I came out."

The three oil workers all agreed that Mr. Mac-
Gruder had come out very early in the morning on the
supply boat to make his usual weekly inspection of the
drilling equipment.

"I'm not doing any smuggling," MacGruder said,
"but I've been very suspicious that something is going
on. The damaged equipment out here, the tampering
with Crowe's boat, those Connors brothers starting
trouble at the wharf, the way Mr. Hanley seems
almost to be provoking the protesters, that Yamura
sneaking around on his own all the time—everything
points to some kind of plot."

"Do you think," Jupiter asked, "that Mr. Hanley
could have some private scheme?"

"I don't know," Mr. MacGruder said. "He's always been highhanded with people who get in his way, so maybe he's just being his normal self with the protesters. But I'm suspicious of the Connors brothers and Yamura. I've been watching them whenever I get the chance. I saw the brothers board the *Sea Wind,* so I trailed them to that tavern and asked them what they were up to!"

"*You* followed *them*?" Pete exclaimed. "Then they were lying! Their whole story was phony!"

"So it seems," Jupiter said. "What about Yamura, sir?"

"I asked him what he was doing in that bar," Mr. MacGruder explained. "He said he was observing American ways!"

"Jupe! Maybe he's smuggling stuff from Japan!" Pete cried.

"Perhaps, Second. But I'd say he was too old to be operating that diver's vehicle himself. The Connors brothers are experienced divers, but they were out here on their boat."

"Were they?" Pete exclaimed. "I mean, *both* of them? I don't remember ever seeing Jed at all!"

"But they have their own boat," Mr. MacGruder pointed out. "Wouldn't it be easier just to use their boat to take anything in?"

Jupiter thought a moment. "Easier, yes, but perhaps not so safe."

Mr. MacGruder said, "When this storm is over, I

think you boys should tell the police what you know."

"Yes, sir," Jupiter said, "but perhaps we can do something right now."

"Do what, Jupiter?" Mr. MacGruder asked.

"Well, that diver and his vehicle must still be out here. The *Sea Wind* was his only way back to shore. He might have gone in to the island for safety, but if he's smuggling something from this platform he could be on the platform right now!"

The manager and his men glanced around as if the unknown intruder might leap out at any second.

"Let's find out," Mr. MacGruder said. He instructed the three oil-rig workers to pick up everyone off duty and have them search the crew's quarters and operations rooms for a stranger. With the boys and Captain Jason, he began to search the lowest deck himself.

"I want him found," MacGruder said grimly. "Maybe he's not a smuggler but a saboteur! He could be the one who's been damaging our equipment."

They found no one in the storage and equipment rooms on the lowest deck. But Pete spotted some diving equipment, which he pointed out.

"We have our own divers, Pete," Mr. MacGruder explained, "to inspect the bottom and keep the platform legs clear of marine life."

The off-duty oil men found no one suspicious in the crew's quarters, mess room, recreation room, galley, or operations rooms on the next two decks.

Rain swept the top deck, and the wind shook the steel walls of the deck houses. Safety lines had already been strung across all the open spaces between the machine shop, the drilling rooms, the drilling tower, and the crane hoist. Bolts of lightning from an approaching thunderstorm lit up the darkening day.

MacGruder found slickers for the boys, and along with Captain Jason they helped the crew search the top deck. They found no one hiding there.

The rain slackened, but not the wind. The whole platform was shaking. MacGruder conferred anxiously with the crew chief, then turned to the boys. He had to shout to be heard over the thunder and howling gale.

"The chief says the barometer is still falling! It's going to get a lot worse! We've tried to call shore, but the radio isn't working because of the lightning!"

At that moment an enormous wave broke high on the platform legs, flinging heavy spray across the top deck. "We'd better go below! The wind isn't even at hurricane strength yet, and the waves are already dangerously high. Soon no one will be safe up here!"

Another wave hit, sending a blast of spray over the group on deck. They clung to the safety lines. Pete was turned toward the distant shadow of Santa Cruz Island. Suddenly his face went white.

"Ov . . . over . . . there! Wha . . . what is it?"

No more than half a mile away, where white water churned over Shark Reef, something was rising from the sea! Something dark and large, indistinct in the storm, trailing long tendrils like twisted arms and legs!

"I . . . don't . . . know," Mr. MacGruder answered.

The dark shape seemed to hang in the sky!

"I never saw anything—" Captain Jason began.

A sudden flash of lightning lit the sea and sky. They saw the thing clearly for an instant.

Festooned with dark seaweed, the long black shape towered out of the churning sea like some great sea monster!

15

The Rusted Hulk

"Come in, Shark Reef Number One. Do you read me, Shark Reef? Santa Barbara Coast Guard Station calling Shark Reef Number One. Come in, Shark Reef."

In the silent study of Mr. Crowe's big old house, the voice of the Coast Guard radioman went on and on. It seemed to come out of the storm itself. Bob and Mr. Crowe kept hoping for an answer to the voice, but none came.

"You think they're okay on the platform, sir?" Bob said. He was sitting near the window, watching the heavy rain and the trees bending in the wind.

"I don't know, Bob," Mr. Crowe said. "I expect they are, but a hurricane is a terrible thing, and I won't lie to you."

"Sir? Try the Coast Guard again," Bob urged. "Maybe they know something new. I mean, maybe

they've heard from some boat out there, or from Santa
Cruz Island."

"All of Santa Cruz is owned by one man, Bob.
There's only the one ranch out there. But I'll check."
He sat down at the console. "John Crowe calling
Lieutenant Jameson. Come in . . ."

The receiver responded at once. "Jameson here,
Crowe."

"Anything new, Lieutenant?"

"Negative. I'm sorry."

"What about a report on the platform? From some
ship, or perhaps from Santa Cruz?"

"No reports, Crowe. All the radios must be out
from the electrical disturbance." There was a moment's silence on the radio, then the lieutenant
continued in a less businesslike manner. "They should
be all right, Crowe. Last we heard from Shark Reef
One, everything was secure. They should be in no
danger out there unless the center of the hurricane
hits, and even then they'll probably be fine. Don't
worry, they'll come through okay."

Mr. Crowe clicked off his microphone, stood up,
and walked to the window. The storm's fury seemed
to lash at the big old house. But there was no real
danger here.

"Should we call Rocky Beach?" Bob said.

"Not yet, Bob. No sense worrying their folks
unnecessarily."

"Then what do we do?" Bob wailed.

"We wait," Mr. Crowe said. "And in the meantime, I'll fix some dinner."

"I don't think I *can* eat," Bob said.

"Going hungry won't help you or the people on the platform," Mr. Crowe said. "Now, remember. That platform is very sturdy. It's built to withstand wind and waves."

Bob nodded, but his gaze was distant. He seemed to be trying to see the far-off platform.

On Shark Reef #1, another wave crashed high on the steel legs. Pete, Jupe, Captain Jason, and Mr. MacGruder all stared at the dark shape rising from the sea above Shark Reef.

"It—it's—a sea monster!" Pete stammered in terror.

Squalls of thick rain obscured their view of the object.

"What could it be, MacGruder?" Captain Jason wondered.

"I don't know! I've never seen—"

Another flash of lightning lit up the sea and sky momentarily like day. The black shape still rose out of the waves like the slowly thrusting arm of some swimming giant.

"Wait!" Jupiter said, his voice shaking. "I think . . ."

A bright sheet of lightning flashed once more.

"Yes!" Jupiter cried, almost laughing with relief. "It's not a monster! It's a submarine! An old, rusted submarine covered with seaweed!"

"It's awfully small for a sub," Captain Jason said, staring as hard as he could at the object. "And I never heard of any sunken sub around Santa Cruz!"

"I'm certain—" Jupiter began.

A longer flash than any before illuminated the whole sea, and then they all saw it, high out of the water—a long, thin shape mottled with rust and weed. They made out the bulge of the conning tower. The clear form of an encrusted cannon showed between the conning tower and the narrow bow. As they watched, the thing stopped rising. It seemed to hang in the air. Then, almost in slow motion, it fell half on its side and slid back down all in the same motion and vanished once more beneath the waves surging over the reef.

"It's gone," Pete said, awed.

"And Jupiter was right," Mr. MacGruder said. "It's a submarine."

"A small one," Captain Jason said. "And old. That deck gun—I never saw a sub with a deck gun. And I never heard of any sub sunk on Shark Reef!"

"Well, we saw it. Now—" Mr. MacGruder began.

Before he could go on, the largest wave yet smashed into the trembling platform, breaking over the top deck itself and sending spray high up the drilling derrick. Water swept across the steel deck, threatening to tear the people from their grip on the life lines, and sweep them off into the raging sea.

"Below!" Mr. MacGruder shouted. "Everyone get below!"

The rain was suddenly so heavy they could barely see each other. They struggled along the life lines to the shelter of a deck house and the companionway below. Wave after wave hit the shuddering platform, smashed against the steel legs, and swept across the top deck. Water poured down the steel stairs and along the corridors until the crew on duty managed to close all exterior doors.

Mr. MacGruder, Captain Jason, and the boys made their way to the platform chief's small office. They saw it was now past seven o'clock. They sat in silence and listened to the storm while the platform swayed and shook. In the crew's quarters, the workers lay on their bunks or played cards in the recreation room. As each giant wave crashed against the rig, the card players paused in their game to listen and wait. No one spoke. The only movement was the grim coming and going of the tired, wet crew members who were still manning posts on the storm-lashed top deck.

"Can . . . can the platform . . . take it?" Pete asked.

"I don't know," Mr. MacGruder said. "It's tightly

anchored to bedrock, but it's never been in a storm like this. The hurricane's center must be right on us."

"No," Captain Jason said, "not yet. It's near, but this isn't the worst yet."

Wave after wave hammered the steel platform. It groaned and shuddered. The silence below decks seemed to quiver with fear beneath the violent noise above.

"I've been thinking about that submarine," Jupiter said, talking to break the tension. "It's small, and Captain Jason says it has to be old. It has a deck gun, and submarines don't have them anymore. But submarines did have deck guns at the beginning of World War Two."

Two more giant waves crashed over the top deck.

"You're right," Captain Jason said. He held to the steel wall as the platform swayed. "It must be a World War Two sub. Only we didn't lose any around here that I know of."

Something fell with a roar high above.

"Perhaps," Jupiter went on, keeping his voice steady, "it isn't an American submarine. Perhaps it's Japanese."

"That could explain why I never heard of a sinking," the captain agreed calmly.

Up on the top deck something had broken loose. They could hear the shouts and struggle as the crew fought to control it.

"Sir," Jupiter said, "I remember something about a Japanese submarine attacking the California coast back then. It was the only enemy attack on the mainland of the United States after the War of 1812." He reached into his encyclopedic memory. "I think it happened in February 1942."

"Of course!" Mr. MacGruder exclaimed. "It was just a few months after Pearl Harbor! The Japanese sub surfaced only a few miles from here, near the Ellwood oil field. It was at sunset. The sub fired about twenty-five shots from its deck gun at our shore. Some of the shells landed a mile inland, but the Japanese gunners were bad shots, or nervous, and they didn't hit anything! The sub slipped away in the dark. But I think it was later sunk with all hands in the South Pacific."

A monster wave slammed into the platform. The great steel structure seemed to lean. Small objects fell all around the group in the office. Water trickled down from above.

"Perhaps," Jupiter said, "the sub didn't sink in the South Pacific, but right here on Shark Reef, and the Japanese didn't want anyone to know that! Or perhaps there were *two* subs here."

"Submarines often sailed in teams," Captain Jason said.

Another giant wave crashed on the platform.

"Then," Jupiter said, "perhaps the diver in the

Shark Hunter isn't a smuggler or a saboteur. Perhaps he wants something on that lost submarine!"

"After all these years?" Pete said. "I mean, why wait so long? And how did he know the sub was down there?"

"I think," Jupiter said, "we'll have to get Bob to do some checking as soon as the radio—"

A third monstrous wave slammed into the platform. It swayed far over as if it would fall!

"Hang on!" Mr. MacGruder cried.

The lights went out!

"I'm going up to have a look!" MacGruder said.

"We'll come too!" Jupiter declared.

The boys followed MacGruder up into a deck house and peered out through a heavy porthole. The tall crane was down. The rain was so heavy they couldn't see the derrick. White-topped waves that seemed as high as the platform rolled in from the south. As the boys watched, a wave broke against the platform and sent tons of water crashing over the top deck. The platform shook.

"I don't know how long we can take this!" Mr. MacGruder cried.

Silently, Pete and Jupiter looked out at the great storm and wondered if they would survive the night.

16

Bob Makes
a Discovery

Bob opened his eyes. He sensed that something was wrong!

He was lying on the couch in Mr. Crowe's cluttered study, where he had spent the night. He tensed and listened hard. Slowly he raised his head to look around the dim room.

There was no sound anywhere—only silence in the big old house and outside.

The storm had passed!

Bob jumped up and ran to the window. He pulled back the drapes, and a dazzling low sunlight filled the study.

"Mr. Crowe! The storm's over!"

In the chair by the radio Mr. Crowe woke up. He sat up, confused.

"What? What is it, Bob! What's wrong?"

"The storm, sir! It's gone!"

Mr. Crowe blinked in the early-morning light, then jumped up and hurried to join Bob at the window. Outside, the trees still dripped rain, and the yard was a shambles of broken branches, palm fronds, debris, and large puddles. But the wind had vanished and the sunlight, piercing through broken clouds, made the wet landscape sparkle.

"Call the Coast Guard, sir!" Bob cried.

Mr. Crowe turned to the transmitter/receiver. As he did, it began to crackle on the *Sea Wind*'s frequency. "*Sea Wind* calling Mr. Crowe! Come in, please. *Sea Wind* calling . . ."

"That's Jupiter!" Bob exclaimed.

Mr. Crowe bent to the microphone. "Jupiter! Crowe here. Are you all safe?"

"Is everyone okay?" Bob yelled.

On the battered platform, Jupiter grinned when he heard Bob's voice. Pete stood at the window of the radio room looking out at the toppled crane, broken and twisted railings, buckled deck plates, and all the other damage of the violent storm. The sea still rolled in huge slow swells that shook the platform.

"Yes, sir," Jupiter said into the radio, "we're all fine. We took a bad beating—we had winds over ninety miles an hour—but the platform came through okay."

"You're on the *Sea Wind*? Are you coming right in?"

"No, sir," Jupiter answered. "The *Sea Wind* is afloat but that's about all, and it's half full of water. Captain Jason and some of the oil workers are trying to pump it out now so they can see the extent of the damage. I'm calling on the *Sea Wind*'s frequency because I wanted to talk to you and Bob."

Bob cried, "Have you found something, First?"

"I think so, Records." He told them about the submarine that had risen to the surface in the hurricane, and about his deductions. "If it is a Japanese submarine from World War Two, it could be what our hitchhiker is really after."

"You don't think he's a smuggler?" Mr. Crowe asked.

"I'm not sure," Jupiter admitted. "If he is, he should have been hiding on the platform. We could have missed him, but my hunch is that he never was on the platform. And if he is looking for that old submarine, that would explain why he studied your charts of the islands and the reefs!"

"What could be on that sub, Jupiter?" Mr. Crowe wondered. "And how did he know it was out there on the reef?"

"That's what we don't know. Pete thinks maybe the sub was carrying gold or some other treasure, and someone just found out."

"What do you want us to do, First?" Bob said eagerly.

"Go to the library as soon as it opens, Bob, and find

the full story of the Japanese submarine that shelled us in the war. See if there is any hint of some treasure, if the sub could have been sunk off Santa Barbara, or if there could have been *two* subs back then."

"I'll find out," Bob said.

"And," Jupiter continued, "search through the newspapers to see if anything happened recently that might have informed someone that the sub was out here."

"Right," Bob replied.

"What will you two do out there?" Mr. Crowe asked, his voice uneasy.

"Help repair the *Sea Wind,* and watch for any signs of the diver and his Shark Hunter," Jupiter said. "And when the sea calms a little—dive down and find that submarine!"

In the sunny study Mr. Crowe looked at Bob in alarm. The records man of the Investigator team bit his lip nervously. Mr. Crowe bent to the microphone again.

"Jupiter, that's not an easy dive," he said slowly. "Not in this weather. The bottom will be all churned up, and that reef can be dangerous. Not just because of the sharks, either. If you dive, be sure Mr. MacGruder or Captain Jason or some other experienced divers are with you all the time. You understand?"

"It's not very deep on the reef, sir, and we'll wait until Mr. MacGruder says it's safe," Jupiter answered.

"All right, but tell MacGruder I want to talk to him when he has the time," Mr. Crowe said.

Jupiter acknowledged and signed off.

In his big house, Mr. Crowe nodded to Bob. "We'll get some breakfast, and then you can go to the library. While you're gone, I'll call your father. He can tell Pete's and Jupiter's families that the boys are fine."

They had a quick breakfast of ham and scrambled eggs, and Bob hurried downtown to the main library. The sun was bright, but all around the city heavy clouds still towered in the sky, and the streets ran with water. Trees were down on many streets, yards were quagmires of mud, and Mission Creek was flowing up to its banks in a roaring torrent.

At the library, the librarian knew of no news stories about a submarine, but he had four books with references to the submarine attack on the county. The accounts were all essentially the same. There was no hint that the sub carried anything of value, but in one book there was some indication of doubt as to how the sub had escaped, or even that it had!

Bob read the story carefully. It said that the sub had seemed to escape northwest toward Point Concepcion, but that the intensive air search had revealed no trace of it, and that there had been a vague report of a possible sighting near Santa Cruz Island to the southwest! Excited, Bob returned the books to the desk.

"Young man," the librarian said. "I believe there *was* something about an old submarine a few months ago in the *Sun-Press*. Some divers or fishermen had some story. If you want to look it up, the paper is on microfilm. The viewers are in the rear."

Bob got the microfilm of the *Sun-Press* for the last year, and began to scan it in the microfilm reader. He found the item three months back. It was a short article buried on an inside page.

WW II JAPANESE SUB FOUND BY DIVERS

Santa Barbara (AP)—The hulk of what appeared to be a Japanese submarine of World War II vintage was sighted yesterday on the ocean bottom off Santa Cruz Island by oil-company divers surveying the area for a new drilling platform.

A Navy spokesman said the Navy has no record of a sub sunk in the area, but that they will study captured Japanese documents and probably send a team to investigate later this year.

Bob quickly unloaded the microfilm from the reader and stood up to return it. Someone behind him blocked his way!

"Interesting story," Tim Connors said. "There's a back door over there, kid. Use it—quietly."

Bob tried to run. Tim Connors caught him by the arm. He opened his mouth to yell for help. The diver's hand clamped over his mouth. He felt something hard against his ribs.

"Nice and quiet," Connors growled. "Walk out that door like I said. We're taking a little ride."

Half-dragged, Bob was hustled out into an alley at the rear of the library. A gray Ford waited there, with Jed Connors at the wheel.

17

The Enemy Revealed!

Pinned to the back seat of the gray Ford by Tim Connors, Bob tried to see where he was being taken. He looked out at the unfamiliar streets—but they *weren't* unfamiliar! Bob was sure he had been this way before.

"Next block, Jed, second driveway," Tim Connors said to the driver. "Pull it all the way to the back of the house."

The gray car slowed in the next block. Bob sat up, staring. Jed Connors turned the car into a familiar driveway.

They had come to Mr. Crowe's house!

Jed pulled to a stop at the end of the driveway. Tim pushed Bob out of the car and through the back gate to the rear door of the house. Stumbling, the junior detective could only blink in disbelief as the Connors brothers herded him inside to Mr. Crowe's cluttered study.

"Ah, now we are all here," a soft voice said.

Mr. Crowe sat at the big marine radio in the corner. But it wasn't Mr. Crowe who had spoken, or whom Bob gaped at. Standing in the center of the study, a large gun in his hand, was the short, bald Japanese businessman, Mr. Yamura. He smiled at Bob without warmth.

"You will please sit on the couch, young man," Yamura said. "Master Andrews it is, yes?"

"You—you—" Bob stammered. "What do you want?"

"No questions," Yamura ordered. His black eyes glittered. "I have said you will sit down."

He nodded to the Connors brothers. Tim dragged Bob roughly across the room, pushed him down hard on the couch, and slapped him across the face. Bob cried out. Mr. Crowe jumped up. Yamura turned his gun toward the author.

"Sit down, please! We must all first understand that we do not play a game, yes? Then we will all be happy."

"You won't get away with this!" Mr. Crowe raged, but he slowly sat down again.

"Very good." Yamura smiled, and carefully brushed a bit of lint from his elegantly tailored silk suit.

Bob now saw the thin trickle of blood on Mr. Crowe's forehead. The author had not been captured without a struggle.

"You're behind it all!" Bob cried to the Japanese man.

"In Japan," Yamura said, "children do not speak loudly."

"Bob's right, though," Mr. Crowe said, watching Yamura. "You've been spying on us, and sneaking around, and the Connors brothers are working with you! They *were* purposely trying to start a riot on the wharf, and they've been sabotaging the platform!"

Tim and Jed Connors grinned, acknowledging the truth of Mr. Crowe's accusation. But a hard look from Yamura kept them from speaking.

"I'll bet you're after that submarine!" Bob blurted out. "And you don't want anyone to know it! That's why you're trying to get the protest stopped and smuggling a diver out there under Mr. Crowe's boat!"

Mr. Yamura watched his captives. "It is as I thought. You are understanding too much."

"Maybe we should get 'em out of the way," Jed Connors said.

"No," Yamura said, "we have need of them." His eyes glinted dangerously as he addressed Bob and Mr. Crowe. "You will do as I say. Then you will not be harmed. We will release you when our work is finished. To make you know we are very serious, I will explain what we do, yes?"

The Japanese businessman began to pace. "By the listening at your window, I learned the two at sea have seen the diver under the boat. They are waiting for his return. Then comes the typhoon. Perhaps they will be sunk, or the diver will be lost. Most unfortunate."

Bob looked puzzled. "But why would you come here to listen in the first place?"

"There are no questions!" Yamura snapped, and went on pacing. "But this morning my helpers listen to *Sea Wind* radio and know the two at sea are safe—and they know of the submarine! The fat one instructs this one on shore to make search of the library for information on submarine. And fat one says they will dive for submarine! This is not good."

Tim Connors laughed. "He don't want no one to know the story of the sub, see? So he sends me to watch the kid and grab him if he spots too much."

"Talk will stop," Yamura said sharply to Tim Connors. He looked back at Crowe and Bob. "Now we come for three reasons, yes? One, perhaps you two will tell someone what your friends do, perhaps the police or Coast Guard. That I do not want. Two, I wish to hear all that will happen at platform. Three, I do not wish for boy to tell those at sea what he has found at library. I wish him to tell what I say to tell, yes?"

Yamura looked harshly at Bob and Mr. Crowe. "Do as I tell, and soon you will go safe."

Bob and Mr. Crowe said nothing. They looked at each other, and Mr. Crowe nodded slowly. They had no choice but to do what Yamura said—at least for now.

Bob glared at Yamura. "What's so valuable on that sub anyway?" he demanded.

Yamura's face darkened. "There are no questions!"

At that moment the radio began to sputter, and Jupiter's voice came into the room!

"*Sea Wind* calling John Crowe! Are you there, Mr. Crowe?"

Yamura nodded to Crowe, gesturing a warning to be careful of what he said. Mr. Crowe turned on the microphone. "Crowe here, *Sea Wind*. What's up, Jupiter?"

"We've been down trying to repair the *Sea Wind*," Jupiter reported. "It's pumped out, but the damage is too severe to return now. Captain Jason says it'll take at least a day to fix the boat, perhaps longer."

Yamura handed Crowe a note. Crowe read it.

"I think we should tow you in at once, Jupiter."

"Not yet, sir." His voice was excited. "I think we're getting closer to an answer. We had to come on the platform because the *Sea Wind*'s propeller was damaged. Captain Jason just found out why. Someone had entangled a steel net with heavy weights in the blades of the propeller, and when we speeded up to come home, all the blades bent and one broke off! Someone tried to sink us, sir, and I think I know who!"

Crowe looked over at Yamura. The businessman nodded.

"Who, Jupiter?" Crowe asked.

"The Connors brothers," Jupiter said angrily. "They were the last out here with us, and they sailed almost on top of us. One of them must have gone underwater and thrown that net into our propeller!"

"Wouldn't that be very dangerous, Jupiter?" Crowe said.

"Yes, sir, but they're experienced divers, and we were at slow speed. They must be behind the whole thing, and they must have known we spotted that diver. Perhaps they heard us reporting to you by radio. I don't know where they are now, sir, so you and Bob be careful."

"Yes," Mr. Crowe said, "we will be."

"Is Bob back from the library?" Jupiter asked.

Yamura shook his head.

"No, Jupiter, not yet," Mr. Crowe said into the microphone.

"He's taking a long time. Maybe he found something!" Jupiter's voice was eager. "Tell him to call us as soon as he returns. The sea is calming fast out here. We can probably dive after lunch."

Jupiter signed off, and Mr. Crowe shut off the microphone. He turned angrily to Yamura.

"You tried to kill them!"

Yamura shrugged. "They see diver under boat and wait for him to return. Necessary to radio Connors men to damage boat."

Jed Connors smiled proudly. "That was pretty fancy diving I did out there. Even Tim wasn't sure I could handle it. Real risky getting near the propeller in that sea, but you got to take risks sometimes, eh? Yamura said damage 'em, so I did!"

Mr. Crowe looked at Jed Connors with disgust. "So what do we do now?"

"In hour," Yamura said, "Andrews boy will call platform, say he has found no information on submarine. No story of the past, not seen by divers now."

The hour passed. Yamura nodded to Bob. The junior detective went unhappily to the microphone. He'd been desperately trying to think of a means to get a secret message to Jupe. But no safe way had occurred to him.

"Calling *Sea Wind*. Bob Andrews calling *Sea Wind*. Come in."

Pete's voice came from the speaker. "Second here, Records. Jupe's down with Mr. MacGruder checking out the diving gear. What'd you find at the library?"

Bob looked at Yamura. "Nothing, Pete. I didn't

find anything we didn't know already."

"Gosh," Pete said, dejected, "we were sure there'd be a story about someone finding the sub. Wait, here's Jupe now."

Jupiter came on. "Nothing, Records? You're sure?"

"I'm sure." Bob kept his voice calm.

"Well, what about that sub back in World War Two? Did you find any accounts of it?"

"Yes," said Bob shortly. He had suddenly thought of a way to signal Jupe that something was wrong.

"Well, what did they say?" demanded Jupe impatiently.

"Nothing new."

"No doubts about the sub escaping? No hint of treasure? No hint of a second sub?"

"No, nothing."

"And you say there weren't any recent reports of finding that sub on Shark Reef?" Jupe asked.

"That's right."

Bob held his breath, hoping that Yamura had noticed nothing strange in this conversation.

Jupiter spoke again, sounding disappointed. "If no one knew the sub was on the reef, then no one could be diving after it. I guess we were wrong."

In the study, Yamura and the Connors brothers smiled.

"But," Jupiter suddenly went on, "I'm convinced

now that the diver isn't a smuggler or a saboteur! He never came on the platform, and he studied those charts of the islands and reefs for a reason. We'll go ahead and dive to the sub anyway!''

Bob grinned. "Sure, Jupe! Go ahead!''

"We'll call you as soon as we return!''

The radio went silent, and Yamura scowled at Bob. The Investigator felt his heart leap. Had Yamura detected his ruse?

"So, they will dive, yes?" the Japanese businessman said. "Then we will wait to hear what they find. Perhaps it is not bad, they will do our work for us, yes?''

Yamura's expression changed to a satisfied smile. Bob realized he was safe. Now if Jupe had only gotten his message!

18

The Secret of Shark Reef

On Shark Reef #1, Jupiter frowned as he and Pete left the radio room to cross the open deck and go below.

"Did you hear anything strange in Bob's voice, Second?"

The platform crew had cut loose the toppled crane and let it drop into the sea. Now they were busy restoring order to the top deck, which swayed gently above the long, rolling swells of the blue ocean.

"He sounded a little down," said Pete. "I guess he felt bad about finding nothing."

"Perhaps. But it was odd that we had to pry information out of him. He didn't volunteer anything! Usually he talks a blue streak when he makes a report."

"Yeah, but usually he really has a lot to tell us,"

Pete pointed out. "I think he was just disappointed."

"Yes, I suppose so," Jupiter conceded.

By now they had reached the bottom deck, and Jupe had other things to think about besides Bob's strange, monosyllabic conversation. The boys found Mr. MacGruder working over the scuba-diving equipment. The thin oil-company manager looked up as they entered the storage room.

"All ready to go," he said. "What did Bob find out?"

"Nothing!" Pete said.

"But," Jupiter added, "I'm still convinced that the submarine is the key to everything. I think we must go down and investigate."

"All right," Mr. MacGruder agreed.

After a break for lunch and a further wait for the sea to calm some more, they carried the scuba gear up to the top deck.

"Since the *Sea Wind* is out of action," Mr. MacGruder said, "our only boat is the diver's boat. Luckily it has its own davits, since we lost the crane."

Jupiter blinked at the open steel-bottomed outboard motorboat that hung from davits at the edge of the deck. Long and seaworthy, it still seemed like a canoe compared to the *Sea Wind*.

"We'll need three divers to be safe, and one man to handle the boat while we're down," Mr. MacGruder decided. "Pete is an experienced diver, and I'll get one of our divers to go down with him and myself. Jupiter can handle the boat."

Jupiter stared at the small boat, and then down at the long swells of the still-heaving ocean.

"I . . . I think, sir," he said nervously, "Captain Jason could handle the boat much better than I, and since I'm not a very experienced diver, perhaps I should stay on the platform."

Pete grinned. "You do look kind of green, First."

"You're right, Jupiter," Mr. MacGruder said solemnly, but his hand covered a smile. "It's better for you to stay near the radio in case your friend Bob has some important news."

"Besides, he might sink the boat!" Pete giggled.

The overweight First Investigator glared at Pete, and Mr. MacGruder went below to get Captain Jason. When they returned, the three divers got into their wetsuits and scuba gear. The oil-company diver, Samuels, put extra tanks and a long equipment bag into the boat, and the oil crewmen lowered it to the water. It heaved and rolled as the four men slid down ropes and took their places in it. Captain Jason started the motor, and they were off.

Pete sat forward in the sturdy little boat which took the long rolling swells well. Mr. MacGruder sat behind him, and they set their course to the reef by lining up landmarks on Santa Cruz Island with the platform derrick.

"Jupiter and I gauged the distance to the sub to be about half a mile, give or take," Mr. MacGruder said. "And Jupe noticed the sub was on a line between the platform and that high headland next to the small cove on Santa Cruz. According to the charts, that should put the sub almost exactly on the southern edge of Shark Reef."

"It may have shifted some in the storm," Pete said.

"Our best bet would be to anchor right on the reef in the line and search seaward," Samuels suggested. "That way we can move in wide sweeps from shallow to deeper water."

They all agreed. The small boat covered the distance from the platform quickly. Pete noticed a sudden sharp change in the sea as they approached the reef. The long swells gave way to a more turbulent choppiness, with white breakers a few hundred yards ahead.

"We're on the reef," Captain Jason said. "It rises fast and almost surfaces ahead there. Give me an exact spot."

Mr. MacGruder and Pete lined the boat up between the platform and the headland on Santa Cruz, and the captain dropped the anchor. There was less than twenty feet of water. Samuels opened the long equipment bag and took out three heavy spear guns.

Pete gulped. "The sharks! I forgot them!"

"There *are* sharks on the reef," Mr. MacGruder

said, "but no more than along most ocean shores. Most of them here aren't really dangerous. The worst sharks are usually out in the open sea, but it's always wise to be prepared."

"Yes, sir." Pete nodded. "I've dived around reefs before."

"Good. We'll all stay together. If you see a shark, get behind me or Samuels and don't make any sudden moves. The worst thing is to panic. Most sharks won't bother us at all."

Pete nodded again. The three divers put on their air tanks, fitted on their masks and mouthpieces, and tumbled backward into the sea.

They swam down slowly. The turbulence calmed as they went deeper, but the water was dark and murky after the hurricane. Pete could see the sharp rock ridges of the reef, with hundreds of small fish swimming in and out of the crevices. The divers swam in long sweeps, working their way deeper as the reef sloped away sharply to the south, toward the platform.

The water grew clearer as they went deeper, and Pete saw the first shark! It was small and dark, swimming slowly near the bottom not fifty feet ahead. Mr. MacGruder touched Pete, smiling over his air tube and shaking his head. Pete got the message—it wasn't a dangerous shark. It soon swam off without coming near.

The divers continued swimming, first to the right and then to the left, still going down, and searched the clearer water for any sign of a submarine. There were more fish, traveling alone or in small schools, and Pete spotted three spiny lobsters scuttling past. Mr. MacGruder pointed to abalone in their heavy shells clinging to the rocks. Giant scallops swam in zigzags, and crabs walked sideways across the edge of the rocky reef. Seaweed grew everywhere like a thick jungle, swaying in the currents of the sea.

Then they saw it!

Samuels pointed urgently with his spear gun!

A great black shape loomed in the hazy water. It was covered with weeds and sea life, and its deck gun was thick with rust and barnacles. The old submarine lay almost upright, with its conning tower pointed toward the faint, far-off light of the surface.

Mr. MacGruder motioned to the others to swim closer. As they did, they saw the gaping hole in the sub's side a few yards behind the conning tower. A hole large enough for two men to swim through, its once-jagged edges had been eroded over the long years by rust and the scouring action of sand carried by sea currents. The divers swam slowly forward, and Pete saw something more.

The bow of the old sub, with its dark torpedo-tube openings, angled upward—as if, after so many years, the sub was about to rise and sail away! Pete realized that the illusion of motion was caused by the bow's being five or ten feet off the bottom. It wasn't touching the reef at all!

MacGruder nodded excitedly and pointed to the surface. He touched his air tank, thrust himself upward, and then fell back. Pete understood! The bow of the sub was off the bottom because there was still air inside! The forward compartments were still watertight, closed off in a last desperate struggle by crewmen who had been forward when the sub struck the reef. They had managed to seal a few bulkhead doors. The air trapped inside had given the submarine the buoyancy to rise to the surface last night, pushed by the violent surge of the first hurricane to strike the reef since those long-ago days of war!

The three divers stared at the raised bow, which even now moved gently in the currents of the reef.

And then they heard the noise!

Faint but sharp, traveling clearly through the silent water of the deep, came a metallic tapping!

The sound was tiny but definite—a tapping of metal against metal, and then a scraping of metal against metal.

The sound seemed to come from the submarine itself!

The three divers looked at each other. Their eyes were wide with disbelief and fear, and a sudden horror. Could someone still be alive in the long-forgotten submarine?

And the macabre tapping came again. Louder now,

the sound changed from tapping to the striking of some metal object against heavier metal. It echoed almost hollowly.

Pete turned in the water. The sound wasn't coming from the watertight bow of the submarine, but from the flooded stern—from the gaping hole toward the rear, where water and fish flowed in and out through a moving curtain of seaweed tendrils.

Pete gestured frantically to his companions. The sound wasn't a sea monster or the ghost of a lost submariner! Someone was inside the flooded part of the submarine!

MacGruder and Samuels nodded, and they began to swim back toward the stern.

At that instant a dark shape swam out through the gaping hole—a diver in mask and wetsuit, carrying a covered metal container the size of a large bucket, and a wicked-looking spear gun!

The diver saw them.

In a quick motion, the diver turned and swam toward the top deck of the wrecked submarine.

MacGruder motioned his group to go after him.

Then they saw the second shark!

Larger than the first, the gray shark appeared above the submarine at the same moment the diver reached the top deck. Shark and diver swam straight at each other!

The diver dropped his container and aimed his

spear gun. The shark veered away and circled toward deeper water—and then swung back in a long arc! Pete and his companions froze as the shark swam directly above them. The diver ahead did not wait for the shark to return, but swam on over the submarine and out of sight on the far side. The shark vanished toward deeper water with a flick of its long tail.

MacGruder and Samuels pursued the diver over the old submarine. Pete retrieved the dropped container, and followed. The three divers saw their quarry climb into his torpedolike underwater vehicle! It *was* the hitchhiker! They swam as fast as they could, but the hitchhiker had too much of a head start and his Shark Hunter was too fast. It disappeared in a swirl of sand.

MacGruder and Samuels stopped in dismay, slowly treading water. MacGruder shook his head, shrugged, and pointed to the surface. Pete nodded—and grinned. He held up the metal container. Behind his diving mask his eyes were triumphant. He was sure that inside the container was the secret of Shark Reef!

19

A Strange
Treasure

The three divers surfaced, and waved to Captain Jason
in the now-distant outboard motorboat. The bearded
captain raised the anchor, started the motor, and came
quickly toward them. The divers clambered aboard
and hurriedly removed their diving gear. Pete reached
for the cylindrical container.

"Let's see what that diver wanted so badly!" he
urged.

"Not yet, Pete," MacGruder said, his eyes searching the surface of the sea. "That diver in the Shark
Hunter could come back anytime, and this boat has a
steel bottom for diving among rocks. If Jupiter is
right and the hitchhiker hooks up magnetically, he
could ride back to the platform with us! Let's move!"

Captain Jason put the motor at full speed, and the
sturdy outboard plunged ahead. Going against the

swell now, it made poorer time, pitching heavily but riding well and taking no water over the bow. Pete fidgeted impatiently as he held the diver's dropped container and stared ahead at the giant platform.

At last they arrived at the platform's landing stage, where the *Sea Wind* was still tied up and being worked on. Leaving Samuels to secure the motorboat, the others scrambled up the narrow steel stairway to the lowest deck and then climbed to the top deck. Jupiter was there waiting for them, a pair of binoculars in his hands.

"What is that container, Second!" he cried at once. "I watched you through the glasses, and saw you bring it up!"

"We don't know yet," Pete said.

"Then open it!" Jupiter cried.

MacGruder and Captain Jason gathered around as Pete opened the container's heavy steel catches and lifted off the cover. He reached into the water-filled cannister and took out a small steel box, heavily corroded and covered with barnacles and seaweed, but still intact and locked!

"There are some markings on it," MacGruder noticed.

Pete took out his diving knife and scraped at the encrustations. The box had been painted black, but most of the paint had eroded, and gray steel showed where Pete scraped. Stamped into the metal itself were Japanese characters and some strange emblem.

"That's the emblem of the Japanese Imperial Navy!" Captain Jason exclaimed. "That box must have belonged to the sub's commander. For official papers!"

Pete broke the lock, and pried open the box. Inside was a thick package wrapped in heavy oilskin and tied securely. There was no water in the box, and the oilskin was in good condition.

"The box is watertight. The Japanese captain must have sealed it," Captain Jason said.

Pete cut the strong binding, which looked more like heavy gut than cord, and unwrapped the package. He took out a small notebook with a heavy canvas cover stamped with the same emblem and more Japanese characters.

"The sub's logbook!" Mr. MacGruder guessed.

Pete opened the book. His face fell.

"It's in Japanese!" he moaned.

Jupiter bit his lip. "Of course, it would be. We'll take it ashore at once. Maybe Mr. Crowe's gardener, Torao, can read it for us. Is there anything else in the box?"

Pete shook his head.

"But there is in the container!" Mr. MacGruder cried as he looked into the canister. He reached in and took out a heavy gold ring. It was engraved with twined leaves and Japanese characters. The characters surrounded a large red gem.

"That's a real ruby, I'm sure," Mr. MacGruder said, "and it's a man's ring. It looks pretty old. A lot older than World War Two. See how the gold leaves are worn smooth?"

They all looked at the logbook and ring in silence. Pete put their unspoken thoughts into words. "Not much of a treasure," he said, disappointed.

"But it's what the diver wanted," Jupiter said.

"And went to a lot of trouble to get," Mr. MacGruder added.

"Unless," Captain Jason said, "he took those things to prove he'd been down there, or as souvenirs, and the real treasure is still in the sub!"

Jupiter shook his head. "No, I don't think he took the box and ring at random, or found them by accident. He must have known exactly what he wanted and where it would be. In fact, I'd say someone on that submarine was *wearing* the ring, and our diver took it off a skeleton!"

"Then maybe," Pete cried, "the logbook and ring are just clues to where the real treasure is!"

"That could very well be," Mr. MacGruder said. "Jupiter is right. You must take the logbook and the ring ashore at once. We'd better radio your friend Bob and Mr. Crowe."

"We'll have to use the motorboat," Pete said. "Better tell Samuels not to hoist it aboard." Pete grinned. "I mean, if Jupe wants to risk riding in the boat this time."

Jupiter gulped, but his round face looked determined. "At least I won't have to slide down a rope to get into it!"

Laughing, they all hurried over to the radio room.

Bob still sat on the couch in Mr. Crowe's study. Mr. Crowe slumped in the chair by the marine radio, and Yamura paced back and forth. The Connors brothers yawned and fidgeted through the long wait.

"*Sea Wind* calling Mr. Crowe! Come in, Crowe!"

Yamura whirled in his pacing, Tim and Jed Connors came awake, and Bob and Mr. Crowe looked at the radio. Yamura motioned sharply to Mr. Crowe to respond to the call.

"Crowe here. Is that you, Jupiter?"

"Yes, sir," Jupiter said. "We're coming in!"

From the distant oil platform, Jupiter went on to tell all they had found in the dive down to the sub.

"The diver must have weathered the storm on Santa Cruz Island, and he's still out here, but I think we have what he is after! Meet us at the marina, and bring Torao."

Mr. Crowe looked at Yamura, who nodded.

"He's not scheduled to come to work today," Mr. Crowe said as Yamura watched him closely, "but I'll go to his rooming house and get him."

"Good, sir. Signing off now. We're coming in right away in the platform's outboard motorboat!"

The radio became silent. Mr. Crowe bit his lip, and suddenly bent toward the mike. Yamura aimed his gun straight at Crowe.

"Do not, please," the Japanese said coldly.

Bob cried, "Mr. Crowe!"

"Shut up!" Jed Connors snarled, and covered Bob's mouth with his hand.

Mr. Crowe sat back slowly in his chair. Yamura nodded to Tim Connors.

"Tie them up!"

The Connors brothers tied and gagged the captives in chairs far from the radio, and the three intruders walked out. Outside, their car drove away toward the harbor. Bob struggled to free himself, but the Connors brothers had tied him too expertly. His eyes pleaded with Mr. Crowe to do something—Jupe and Pete were coming in with the logbook and ring, and Yamura knew it!

Mr. Crowe looked toward the radio. He tried to rock his chair across the floor, but it wouldn't move. Then he knocked himself over sideways and tried to inch across the floor to the radio. He couldn't. He tried to get up again. He couldn't. He lay helpless, unable to move.

Pete and Jupiter waved as the motorboat moved away from Shark Reef #1. Pete steered the sturdy open craft over the powerful swells. Jupiter looked a little green. As Pete headed them straight toward the east end of Santa Cruz Island, where they would turn for home, he started to talk.

"Jupe? You think I'm right about the logbook and ring being clues to a real treasure hidden somewhere? Maybe gold or something from the war, and the sub captain knew where it was?"

"That's possible, Second," Jupiter said shakily. The heaving of the small boat made him hang on to the gunwales.

"I think that's got to be the answer," Pete went on, trying to distract Jupiter from thinking about the lurching of the boat. "What else could the logbook and ring mean?"

"Well," Jupiter said weakly, "they could mean something *private,* nothing to do with treasure at all." His voice grew stronger as he warmed to his own ideas. "I mean, I've been thinking. The value of the logbook has to be that it will tell what happened on the submarine back then. The ring could be a way of identifying someone. So perhaps what the diver is after is proof that someone was on the submarine when it was sunk, and of what happened on it before it was sunk."

Pete smiled as Jupiter's voice livened. They were halfway to the end of Santa Cruz Island now, and . . . Pete swung the rudder full over, and the small boat tipped dangerously and turned sharply right! Jupiter jumped forward and leaned over to fend off the jumble of floating debris Pete had swerved to avoid. There were two large logs and a whole tree that had been torn up by the hurricane.

"That was close," Pete said as he steered slowly past the heavy debris, "but you sure look a lot better all of a sudden!"

Pete was right. Jupiter's color was back, and his eyes were alert. The distraction of talking and the excitement of the near collision had made Jupe completely forget the sickening motion of the heaving boat. But he was annoyed.

"I was perfectly all right all along," he said stiffly.

"Sure you were." Pete grinned.

Miffed, Jupiter stared ahead to the end of Santa Cruz Island and to the gap beyond that would lead them into the Santa Barbara Channel. Then he looked toward the rugged shore of Santa Cruz Island itself, watching it pass. Suddenly he turned to Pete.

Pete was pale. "Yes. I noticed. We've slowed down—a lot!"

"Some of that debris got caught under the boat?" Jupiter asked.

"T-take . . . a look," Pete stammered.

Jupiter sat unmoving for a moment. Then he leaned as far out over the side as he could to look under the boat. The sea was dark and murky from the hurricane—but he saw it!

"It's there, Pete," he whispered. "I can barely see it—about half as long as the boat, attached right in the middle, and dark like a torpedo. It's the Shark Hunter!"

The two boys looked at each other, scared.

"He must have hooked on when we slowed for that debris," Jupiter realized. "Pete! Somehow, he must have planned it!"

They were alone in an open boat twenty miles from the mainland with the diver only a few feet away beneath them!

"He can climb up anytime!" Jupiter cried.

"No, not while we're moving," Pete said. "I could turn fast and leave him out here without his Shark Hunter. He has to wait until we get to shore, but with him under there adding drag to the boat, we'll never have enough gas to reach Santa Barbara!"

They were at the gap between the islands now, and Pete turned into the shelter of the channel.

"We'll have to head for a nearer point onshore," Pete went on. "Down between Santa Barbara and Ventura."

Jupiter nodded, and Pete turned again and headed across the broad channel to the closest land they could see. Suddenly, the boat seemed to speed up again.

"He's helping us!" Pete exclaimed. "He's turned on his motor. It's not a lot, but it's helping!"

"Because," Jupiter said slowly, "we're going where he wants us to go—away from Santa Barbara to an empty stretch of coastline!"

20

The Black Boat

Jupiter and Pete watched the deserted shoreline ahead. Less than half a mile from land now, they could see the rocky headlands, the white beaches, and a long oil pier jutting out into the sea. There were only a few scattered houses on the headlands, and no one was on the beaches.

"It's only five o'clock," Pete said. "Where is everyone?"

"At home, I guess," Jupiter said. "It's still too rough for swimming or surf fishing."

"He'll have us alone!" Pete cried.

"No," Jupiter said. "Highway 101 runs along the shore down here, not fifty feet back. As soon as we land we'll run for the highway. There's heavy traffic at this hour, and he won't dare try to get the logbook and ring away from us in full view of other people!"

Pete nodded. "I'll bring her in to that oil pier. There's a landing stage. We can get up onto it and run along the pier. There ought to be some people on the pier."

The two boys watched the shore and the pier tensely. They guessed that down in the water under them the diver was waiting with equal tension.

They soon passed a long headland to the west and glided through the calmer waters in its shelter toward the long pier. Rocker arms pumped all along the pier, looking like giant birds continually bending down to eat or drink and then rising again. But there was no human being anywhere on the whole long pier, and no cars parked back where the pier joined the land.

"That's funny," Pete said. "There's usually *someone* around an oil pier, even after five o'clock."

"It doesn't matter, Second," Jupiter said. "Highway 101 is just over that ridge up from the beach."

The sturdy outboard held its course, and the boys could see the landing stage directly ahead at the end of the pier. Pete kept the boat at full speed until they were almost on top of the pier. Then he suddenly cut the throttle, swung the boat sharply, and slid into the landing stage with hardly a bump.

"Let's go!" he yelled.

They leaped off the boat without bothering to tie it up, and raced up the wooden stairs to the broad deck of the pier itself. As they reached the top, Pete glanced back and suddenly gasped.

"Jupe!"

Jupiter whirled. The Connors brothers' black boat was speeding straight toward the pier! It must have been hidden by the long headland and had come around the point while the boys were busy with their plans for landing. They could see Jed Connors in the bow and Tim Connors at the wheel on the flying bridge—and someone else next to Tim. A small man in a dark suit and tie.

"That's Mr. Yamura!" Pete cried. "Jupe, they can help us catch the diver!"

"Perhaps," Jupe hesitated.

The black boat was close now, and still moving very fast. The boys' outboard motorboat had drifted out from the landing stage and was in the path of the big black fishing boat.

"It's not going to stop!" Pete cried.

The black boat smashed directly into the motorboat, cut it almost in half, and passed on over it toward the landing stage!

"Jed's got a gun!" Jupiter cried. "Run, Pete!"

The boys raced along the pier toward the shore. There were angry shouts behind them from the still-moving black boat. The boys ran on without looking back.

"Now I'm sure it was the Connors brothers who damaged the *Sea Wind,*" Jupiter panted, "and Yamura is behind everything! He wants that logbook and ring! He sent the diver in the Shark Hunter to get it!"

"They don't even care about that diver!" Pete puffed. "They ran over our boat on purpose, and their diver could still have been under it!"

"Yes, but they *know* the diver doesn't have the logbook and ring!" Jupiter said, gulping for breath. "Now I see why Bob talked so oddly on the radio! He was trying to warn us! Yamura and the Connors brothers must have been there in the study. So they know we're bringing the ring and book to shore!"

The boys reached the end of the pier, ran on over the ridge between the beach and Highway 101, and stumbled down to the edge of the eight-lane freeway.

They stood paralyzed.

It was just after 5:00 P.M., the height of the rush hour, but the broad highway was completely deserted in both directions!

There were no cars and no people. Nothing moved anywhere as far as the eye could see. Silent and empty, the great highway might have been on a planet destroyed by a final war.

In the study of Mr. Crowe's house, the two prisoners heard a car stop in the driveway. Helpless, they listened to the footsteps coming slowly around the house toward the back door. They were the steps of a solitary man. Yamura? One of the Connors brothers?

"John?" a voice called. "John Crowe?"

Mr. Crowe struggled against his bonds and tried to make a sound, but only vague grunts came through the gag. There was only silence outside now. Had the caller gone?

"John! What the devil—!"

Captain Max Berg stood in the study doorway. He quickly untied Mr. Crowe and turned to help Bob. Mr. Crowe rubbed the circulation back into his arms and legs.

"What are you doing here, Max?" Crowe asked.

Free, Bob hobbled around the room.

"MacGruder tried to contact you by radio," Berg said. "When you didn't answer, he figured you must have gone to meet those other two boys, so he contacted the Coast Guard. When they said you weren't at the marina, and that those boys hadn't shown up, he had them call the police."

"Pete and Jupiter didn't arrive?" Bob cried.

"No, and there's no sign of them in the channel."

"Yamura must have them!" Bob wailed.

Mr. Crowe quickly explained everything to Captain Berg.

"My people will start a search for the boys," Berg said, "and we'll go to the Coast Guard. There's one big problem," and the captain looked at them grimly. "Highway 101 is completely blocked! Mud slides everywhere, and a bridge out at Ventura. Nothing can get through in either direction!"

Pete and Jupiter stood at the edge of the empty highway. Their expressions were unbelieving. Where there should have thousands of cars pouring past, there was only silence.

"The hurricane must have blocked the freeway, First," Pete moaned. "I think I can see mud and rocks up that way!"

In the distance to the west, the whole side of a mountain seemed to have collapsed across the highway.

"That's why no one was on the beaches or the pier," Jupiter said shakily. "It means no one can help us, Second!"

Already they could hear heavy feet running on the pier.

"What do we do, First?"

"We can't reach those houses on the headland before Yamura and the Connors brothers cut us off," Jupiter decided hurriedly, "and the beaches are too open. We've got no choice!"

Across the highway, steep, rugged brown mountains covered with chaparral and manzanita came down to the edge of the road. Usually dry and rocky, but wet and muddy now, they were cut by narrow canyons. One canyon began directly ahead.

"Let's make that canyon before they see us!" Pete cried.

They ran across the eerie, deserted highway and were just entering the steep little canyon when they heard a shout.

"There they are!"

The Connors brothers and Yamura stood across the highway. Jed Connors held a rifle, and Yamura had a pistol in his small hand.

"Hurry, Pete!" Jupiter urged.

The boys plunged into the narrow canyon. The steep sides closed in, cutting off the sunlight. The boys stumbled ahead through deep shadows, slipping on the muddy adobe soil. Soon the ground became more rocky as it climbed higher, and they ran more easily. The narrow passage twisted back and forth under the steep slopes, and even narrower canyons split off to the right and left.

Then the main canyon forked, and the boys blindly chose to run to the right. That was a mistake. The fork soon came to a dead end against clifflike walls, and the boys lost valuable minutes retracing their steps.

Breathlessly, Pete and Jupe ran up the canyon's left fork. Now they could hear their pursuers behind— stumbling and swearing, but coming steadily closer!

"Hurry, Jupe!" Pete cried, looking back to where his heavy friend struggled upward.

Jupiter was no longer running. He stood frozen, looking ahead past Pete.

"Pete . . ."

Not ten feet away, a man in a dark wetsuit and diving mask stood pointing a spear gun at them!

At the Coast Guard station Mr. Crowe paced back and forth, and Bob stood at a window watching the darkening sea. Lieutenant Jameson was reading the latest report. He shook his head.

"I'm sorry," he said wearily, "no sign of them yet."

"Where could they be?" Crowe raged. "Unless Yamura *does* have them!"

"No sign of the Connors boat either," Lieutenant Jameson said, and hesitated. "But the Connors brothers and Yamura were seen sailing out of the harbor on it about two hours ago."

Bob and Mr. Crowe said nothing.

"Our cutter is sweeping the channel, and the police helicopters are searching the shoreline and the channel," the lieutenant said. "We'll find them."

"If it isn't too late!" Bob said.

21

Captured!

Pete and Jupe gulped. They'd been caught by the hitchhiking diver!

The Investigators stared hard at him, but all they could see was that he was small and slender. His diving mask and wetsuit hood hid his face in the deep shadows of the canyon.

The diver motioned with his spear gun. He wanted Pete and Jupiter to turn into a side canyon that was little more than a narrow barranca. The Investigators hesitated. The diver again motioned sharply with the spear gun.

"Okay, okay," Pete muttered.

The boys plunged into the darkness of the narrow side canyon. The diver prodded them forward and up a sharp curve until they reached a small ledge. The diver motioned for them to lie down on the ledge. It overlooked a canyon, and the boys realized that they were now looking down into the same canyon they had just left, at almost the exact spot where they had been captured!

The diver knelt behind them, and signaled that they were to be quiet. The boys were puzzled, but they didn't have to be told again. They could hear Yamura and the Connors brothers panting and cursing in the canyon below. The men came closer and finally emerged directly beneath the ledge—and stopped. Their voices rose clearly in the early evening air.

"What're we stoppin' for?" Jed Connors demanded below.

"Something is wrong," Yamura said.

"Hey, come on! We're gainin' on 'em!" Tim Connors exhorted.

"And we could hear them," Yamura's voice rose from below. "Now we do not hear."

"These small canyons play tricks with sound," Jed Connors growled. "They can't be far ahead now! Come on!"

The pursuers vanished on up the canyon with Yamura in the rear, looking like a man deep in thought. The diver prodded Pete and Jupiter, and motioned toward a narrow mountain track that led higher and south toward the ocean again! The boys slid and scrambled along the muddy, rocky trail, which skirted dangerous abysses.

At last they emerged on a high bluff. In the evening light they could see the channel, the long oil pier, and the eerie, deserted superhighway far below. The black boat with the flying bridge bobbed alone at the end of the pier. A helicopter suddenly appeared, flying low from somewhere inland. The diver made the Investigators crouch motionless. The helicopter swooped low over the black boat, and then disappeared to the west.

The diver motioned toward a cluster of large boulders at the top of the bluff. Pete and Jupiter climbed up. The rocks formed a rough circle with a clear view in all directions and a sheltered recess inside protected from the wind. The diver prodded Pete and Jupiter into the low, sheltered niche, and crouched facing them. He spoke for the first time.

"We should be safe here for the night," he said sharply. "Now you can give me back my logbook and my ring!"

Captain Max Berg strode into the Coast Guard station.

"We've spotted the Connors brothers' boat."

Bob leaped up from the chair where he had been brooding as dusk fell over the sea and the marina. Mr. Crowe and Lieutenant Jameson stopped conferring and looked at the policeman.

"I just had a report from one of our helicopters," Berg went on. "The boat's tied up at the end of an oil pier about twelve miles southeast, between here and Ventura. There didn't seem to be anyone aboard it, and the pilot saw no trace of a motorboat."

"We have to go down there!" Bob cried.

Captain Berg shook his head. "The chopper pilot saw no one anywhere in the area. Not on the pier, on the highway, or near the few houses in the area. He says it's so deserted down there now that he could have seen a lizard cross the highway. So he's sure that if anyone is down there at all, they're in the mountains."

"And we'd never locate anyone in those mountains at night," Mr. Crowe realized.

"No," Lieutenant Jameson agreed. "We'll have to wait until morning."

"But those crooks could have Pete and Jupe and the stuff from the submarine," Bob cried, "and they'll get away!"

"I don't think so," Captain Berg said. "The highway is completely blocked, we've got patrol cars at each end of the blocked section, and there's no other road out. They can't get far through the mountains at night, and the Highway Patrol is watching Route 33 on the other side of the mountains."

"I'll take the cutter and anchor offshore so they can't escape in the boat," Lieutenant Jameson said.

"Bob and Crowe can sleep on the cutter. In the morning, we'll go after them."

Inside the circle of boulders, Pete and Jupiter reluctantly handed the ring and logbook to the masked driver. Pete glared at the man.

"Who are you? Why don't you take off that mask?"

"He doesn't have to, Second," Jupiter said. "I know who he is!"

"Who, Jupe?" Pete cried.

"Torao," Jupiter said. "Mr. Crowe's gardener!"

The diver removed his diving mask. It *was* Torao!

"When did you figure it out, Jupiter?" the youthful Japanese gardener asked, smiling at the stout leader of the Investigators.

"I should have known from the start," Jupiter said angrily. "When Mr. Crowe called you his *new* gardener, and you were there when that intruder escaped us in Mr. Crowe's backyard. You simply hid, let us run past you, got out of your wetsuit, and pretended you'd just been there gardening! You lied about seeing two men to fool us. *You* were the person in Mr. Crowe's study!"

"Yes," Torao admitted. "I had to check Mr. Crowe's protest schedule book to know when he planned to take the *Sea Wind* out, and I needed to study the charts of the reefs to know where to search for that submarine."

"And you're not working with Yamura and the

Connors brothers," Jupiter continued. "They're your enemies!"

The Japanese youth nodded, and sat down inside the circle of boulders. "My full name is Torao Yamura. Mr. Yamura is my grandfather. Or he's supposed to be!"

"Hey!" Pete gaped at Torao. "What happened to the way you talk? I mean, you speak English almost as good as me!"

"Better!" Jupiter grinned.

Torao laughed. "You liked my Mr. Moto act? I've studied English since I was seven, and I went to college at U.C.L.A., but I figured people would pay less attention to a poor gardener who could speak only broken English and didn't understand what was said."

Jupiter asked, "What do you mean by saying Mr. Yamura is *supposed* to be your grandfather?"

"That's what it's all about, Jupiter," Torao said grimly. "My great-grandfather was an ordinary man who learned engineering and founded an oil and chemical company. He was rich, and had only one child, a son. Just before World War Two they had a big fight, and the son left home, got into some trouble, and joined the Imperial Navy. His name was Shozo Yamura. He was in the navy for the whole war, was wounded many times, and was finally captured. He didn't return to Japan until 1946."

There was a sound in the hills! They all listened,

but it didn't come again. Pete peeked over the boulders but couldn't see anyone. Torao went on.

"My great-grandparents and almost all of their relatives died at Hiroshima in the war. There were some cousins left, but Shozo was the only heir, so when he came home he got the whole fortune and the company."

"But," Jupiter said, "you don't think he was really Shozo!"

"My father never believed it," Torao said. "The man who returned was like Shozo Yamura, but not exactly. He knew much about the family, but not all. He blamed the discrepancies on the eight years' absence and on his war wounds, which changed his face and ruined his memory. All Shozo's records were destroyed in Hiroshima—family, medical, dental, everything—and all the navy records said the man who returned *was* Shozo. Even his fingerprints matched those on record!"

"Fingerprints can't lie, Torao," Pete said.

"But liars can take fingerprints," Jupiter said. "Your father was born *before* the war? Before Shozo went away?"

"Yes. When Shozo left home, he married a poor waitress and my father was born, but they never saw Shozo for the whole war. Of course, my father was too young before the war to remember the man who went away. But he never accepted the man who came back—he disliked him on sight. His mother—my grandmother—hinted that the Shozo who returned was an impostor."

"Then why didn't she expose him?" asked Jupiter.

"She was terrified of him, she couldn't prove anything, and she needed someone to take care of her and her child. Life was very hard after the war, and food was scarce. I guess she decided it was safer to go along with the man. She was wrong!"

Torao glared into the failing light. "The man who calls himself Shozo Yamura is an evil man! In Japan he is hated, and suspected of many criminal activities. He has forced every Yamura relative out of the company, and we suspect him of taking the profits and hiding them so there will be nothing left of the Yamura fortune. He has always lived apart from the family, and he may even have murdered my grandmother—his supposed wife—who died soon after his return!"

"But," Pete wondered, "what happened to your real grandfather?"

Torao was grim. "That's what my father tried to discover when he grew up. He found out that when Shozo left home, he fell in with a gang of juvenile criminals. The leader of the gang, Hideo Gonda, was wanted by the police, and he joined the navy with Shozo! They trained together, and when the war began they were both sent to submarines. Gonda joined a ship, and Shozo went to headquarters onshore. Gonda's submarine went to sea early in 1942 and never returned."

"The two boys changed places!" Jupiter guessed. "It was Shozo who went to sea and was lost, but the navy thought it was Gonda. So, being at headquarters and seeing his chance to escape his past and eventually claim the Yamura fortune, Gonda completely switched the records, even putting his own fingerprints on Shozo's papers. He became Shozo Yamura!"

Torao nodded. "My grandmother once told my father how patriotic Shozo was, and how eager he was to go to sea. He would have hated being stuck in a desk job!"

"Then that sub out there on Shark Reef is Gonda's sub?" Pete cried.

"Yes," Torao said. "We always knew the number of the submarine, and that it had sailed to the American coast, but we never knew for sure where it had sunk. Not until a month ago!"

Torao paused, and then went on. "There was one sure proof against 'Yamura.' Shozo wore a family ring that 'Yamura' said he had lost during the war. My father didn't believe that. He was sure that wherever Shozo died, he was wearing the ring. Last month we saw a story in a Tokyo newspaper about divers finding an old Japanese submarine near Santa Barbara! I came over at once.

"I'm a trained diver. I bought the Shark Hunter and was about to rent a boat when my father cabled that 'Yamura' knew about the sub and was in the States! I knew he'd try to stop me, so I had to hide and somehow dive in secret. I saw the protest boats, and got the idea of riding under the *Sea Wind*. I took the job of Mr. Crowe's part-time gardener to keep out of sight, dove secretly, and located the sub the day of the hurricane.

"But I had to take refuge on Santa Cruz. When the storm passed, I dove again. I found the logbook box, and I found the ring. It was on a small skeleton. I . . . had found my grandfather." Torao's voice was sad. He was silent a moment. "But then you and that shark made me lose the container. I had a small radio ashore, and heard your plans. So I waited under that debris, pushed it into your path, and the rest you know. But the ring, and maybe the logbook, are my proof, and—"

Pete cried softly, "Look! Down there!"

In the narrow canyon below the bluff, a small fire was burning in the twilight. A campfire for warmth in the evening chill!

"It must be Yamura!" Pete cried. "We can escape the other—"

"Wait!" Jupiter exclaimed. "There's another campfire!"

The second small fire was at the edge of the highway in the opposite direction.

"They're trying to trick us," Torao said. "I see no shadows around those campfires. They've guessed we doubled back, but they don't know where we are, and they want us to think we can escape back into the mountains! They're probably really waiting up in the canyons for us. They want to make us move."

"What do we do?" Pete moaned.

"They don't know where we are, so as long as we're quiet we'll be safe here. We had better get some sleep. Tomorrow we can elude them in the daylight and escape!"

22

The Villains
Smoked Out!

Dawn came faintly through the portholes of the Coast Guard cutter as Mr. Crowe shook Bob awake.

"We want to be ashore before sunup," the author said, "so we won't be seen. Breakfast is ready."

Bob dressed quickly, and hurried to the mess room where Mr. Crowe, Lieutenant Jameson, and three Coast Guardsmen were already eating pancakes and sausage. Through the mess-room portholes Bob saw that the cutter was anchored near a headland.

"Where's the Connors boat?" he asked.

"Tied up to a pier on the other side of that headland," answered Lieutenant Jameson. "We anchored here so we'd be hidden. We'll land on the headland and work our way around to the pier. That way no one on the pier, or highway, or in the mountains will be able to spot us."

The launch was ready, and they all boarded it and rode in to a small beach on the headland. Ashore, they moved swiftly through the trees.

Pete awakened in the circle of rocks on the high bluff when the first faint sunlight tinged the eastern sky. He listened, but there was no sound anywhere except the singing of the birds and the faint rustle of small animals in the brush.

"Jupe," he whispered. "Torao."

The Japanese youth, still in his black wetsuit, woke up at once. He nodded to Pete, crawled to the edge of the circle of boulders, and carefully looked all around.

Jupiter groaned, and tried to burrow into the ground and go on sleeping. Pete laughed.

"Nothing like nice rocky dirt for a bed," he said.

Jupiter opened one eye. "I think that every bone in my body is broken."

"A nice breakfast would fix that," Pete grinned. "If we had any breakfast."

"Not to mention lunch or dinner," Jupiter said, and sat up. "The only thing that feels worse than my bones is my stomach."

Torao crawled back. "I don't see any sign of them. Maybe they gave up."

"No," Pete said, looking out to sea. "Their boat's still at the pier. Maybe they slept on it!"

"I hope so," Torao said. "But we have to move now

before it gets too light down in the canyons. The highway is still deserted, so our best route is through the mountains to Highway 33. You fellows had better carry the logbook and ring. I have no pockets."

"I'll put the book under my shirt," Jupiter said. "Pete can take the ring."

"Okay, let's get started," Torao said.

They climbed over the rocks and trotted toward the rear of the high bluff. A voice shouted from far below!

"Torao! We will talk, so?"

Far down at the bottom of the narrow canyon that bordered the bluff, Yamura, who they knew now was really Hideo Gonda, shouted up from beside the still-smoldering campfire.

"We will understand each other, yes?"

Torao started to run along a narrow rocky trail that led down the bluff away from the canyon. Pete and Jupiter plunged after him. The trail curved around the bluff into a broader canyon and then descended through a thick grove of dusty live oaks.

Jed Connors stepped from the grove and caught Torao!

"Gotcha!"

Pete and Jupiter whirled to run. Tim Connors grinned behind them. "Hey, the junior snoopers again." He held a gun.

Bob crouched in the ditch at the edge of the wide, empty highway.

"It was Yamura!" he whispered to the others in the ditch. "In that canyon yelling up at someone! It must have been Pete and Jupe!"

"He went on up the canyon," Mr. Crowe said as he studied the entrance to the narrow cut in the rugged hills. "But I don't see the Connors brothers."

"Let's take a look," Lieutenant Jameson said.

He motioned his men forward. They ran across the highway and entered the steep canyon directly across from the oil pier. Half-crouched, they moved slowly up the silent canyon. The early-morning sunlight failed to reach between the narrow walls, and they worked ahead through deep shadow. Bob pointed to the muddy ground.

"Look! A lot of people have been through here since the storm. All kinds of footprints!"

Lieutenant Jameson studied the ground. "At least five different prints, I'd say."

"Pete and Jupe," Bob cried, "chased by the other three!"

They continued on in the shadows of the narrow canyon. Mr. Crowe spotted the campfire.

"It's still smoldering," he said. "They can't be far!"

Then they heard angry cries and deep laughter somewhere ahead! There was the distant sound of a brief scuffle, and then silence.

"What was that?" Mr. Crowe said uneasily.

"It sounded like . . ." Lieutenant Jameson didn't finish.

"Like Pete and Jupe getting caught!" Bob cried.

Mr. Crowe looked at Lieutenant Jameson.

"I'm afraid it did sound like that," the author said.

"We have to rescue them!" Bob started to run.

"Wait!" Lieutenant Jameson stopped him. "If we try to attack, even let Yamura and his men know we're here, they might . . . hurt the boys."

The rescue party looked helplessly at each other. If they did nothing, Yamura and the Connors brothers could get away! If they tried to stop them, Pete and Jupiter could be in great danger!

"Sir!" Bob said suddenly. "I've got an idea!"

Pushed by the Connors brothers, the three captives stumbled along the steep trail until they came out into the canyon at the same place where Torao had saved the boys last night. Torao was gloomy.

"I'm sorry, fellows," he said bitterly. "I should have known it was a trick. Gonda shouted to make us run the opposite way, where he had his gang waiting!"

"So? You know at last, yes?" another voice said.

Yamura-Gonda came out of the shadows. He laughed at Torao.

"A trick, so? You are stupid. The Yamuras were never so smart, yes? Shozo so patriotic, so much a young fool! He must go to sea and die. The shore and desk much safer, yes?"

The small man laughed again. A nasty laugh.

"You will give me the logbook and ring!"

"We hid them!" Pete said quickly. "Where you won't find them!"

"So?" Yamura-Gonda nodded to the Connors brothers. "Search!"

They stood Torao and the boys with their hands above their heads, leaning forward against the canyon wall. Jed searched Jupiter, while Tim examined Pete. Yamura-Gonda searched Torao himself. Jed took the logbook from under Jupiter's shirt in triumph! Tim continued to search all through Pete's clothes, even taking off his shoes, but he found nothing.

"This one doesn't have any ring," Tim said.

Yamura-Gonda had found nothing on Torao.

"Search again! The fat one also!"

The Connors brothers went through every inch of clothing once more. They found no ring. Yamura-Gonda found nothing. He was furious.

"You will tell where you hide it!"

The boys and Torao stood silent, defiant.

"So? Then we must—"

"Boss?" Jed said suddenly. "Smoke!"

They all looked back down the canyon toward the ocean. Puffs of thick white smoke rose into the bright morning sky. Some short and some long, the puffs seemed to come from the burning of damp leaves or brush.

"Hey," Tim cried, "that's where we built that campfire. We must have left it burning. The wet brush has caught fire!"

"No matter!" Yamura-Gonda dismissed the problem. "Let the fire burn. I must have ring! If you do not tell, I will find ways."

Jupiter was looking toward the smoke. "I . . . don't hurt us, sir! Please! I'll show you where we hid the ring!"

"Jupe?" Pete said.

Torao was puzzled. "But . . ."

"I'll show you," Jupiter said, his voice shaking, "if you let us go!"

"Show me, you go," Yamura-Gonda said quickly.

Jupiter swallowed. "We hid it on the pier when you sank our boat. Before we ran. The book was too big to hide."

Yamura-Gonda was impatient. "Show now!"

The Connors brothers herded the boys and Torao back down the narrow canyon. Soon they saw the deserted highway ahead, the silent pier, and the empty sea. Nothing moved anywhere.

"Lucky the hurricane blocked the road," Jed Connors said.

"But someone will pursue soon," Yamura-Gonda said. "Hurry!"

He pushed to the front, and they all followed him down the last few hundred feet of the canyon.

Mr. Crowe leaped from the bushes and tackled

Yamura-Gonda! The three Coast Guardsmen and Lieutenant Jameson jumped out of hiding and grabbed the two Connors brothers! Quickly disarmed, Tim and Jed shrugged and raised their hands. Bob emerged grinning.

"I figured you'd read my signals," he said to Jupiter.

Yamura-Gonda struggled in Mr. Crowe's grasp.

"Signal?" he raged. "No signal! Hear no signal!"

"Not hear," Bob said, laughing, "see! I sent smoke signals! You left your fire smoldering, and there was plenty of firewood and wet brush to make smoke!"

"Morse code," Jupiter explained trimphantly. "He sent just three letters: B-O-B. His name! They told me that rescuers were near—and exactly where! All I had to do was get you to come down to the campfire. Good work, Records!"

Yamura-Gonda stared in disbelief. The Connors brothers looked almost admiring. Mr. Crowe laughed—and suddenly saw Torao! He stared at the Japanese youth.

"Torao! What are you . . . Wait! You mean he was the diver?"

The whole story was explained to the author. He nodded slowly.

"You tangled with the wrong boys, Yamura," he said. "And the police have some serious charges against you now!"

"Not as serious as those in Japan, Mr. Crowe,"

Torao said, "and do not call this criminal 'Yamura'! He is Hideo Gonda, and the proof of his fraud will be here." He held up the logbook he had taken from Jed Connors, then leafed through it. "Here is one of the last entries by the submarine captain: 'A young seaman named Hideo Gonda has come to me in these our last hours. He says that Gonda is not his name, and he does not wish to die in dishonor with a false name. He is Shozo Yamura; he has a son and family at home. If this record is ever found, he prays that his son and his family will be told that he died in honor as Shozo Yamura.' "

They all listened to the words from so long ago. Torao's eyes were bright now. He had found his real grandfather.

"With this log, and Shozo's ring, Gonda will go to prison," he said, and blinked. "The ring! Pete, you said you had it! Where is it?"

Pete laughed. "The one place no one thinks of looking for a hidden ring."

He held up his right hand. On the ring finger was a large man's ring, half hidden by caked mud.

"They forgot to look at my hand!"

23

Mr. Hitchcock
Pleads Exhaustion

When the highway was cleared, The Three Investigators returned to Rocky Beach. Bob wrote up his account of their adventures at Shark Reef, and once again the boys went to Alfred Hitchcock to ask him to introduce the case.

When he finished reading Bob's account in his plush studio office, the famous movie director wiped his brow. "I am exhausted from simply reading such wild adventures!" the director cried. "What, a hurricane, sharks, submarines, villains, and—horror of horrors—no food for a full day! I shall never set foot upon an oil platform!"

"Jupe even lost a couple of ounces," Pete added, grinning.

"And everything solved with such cleverness and energy," Mr. Hitchcock said. "Morse code in smoke, and a ring hidden in plain sight! Shades of Edgar Allan Poe."

"Pete and Bob really saved the case," Jupiter confessed.

"With the aid of inspired leadership, I'm sure," Mr. Hitchcock said, with a twinkle in his eye. "Now, what of the villains?"

"Jed and Tim Connors are charged with assault, breaking and entering, kidnapping, sabotage, and even piracy on the high seas for trying to sink the *Sea Wind!*" Pete said. "But Captain Berg says they were really duped by Yamura, I mean Gonda. He told them Torao was a criminal trying to destroy evidence against him on that sub. So the bigger charges will be dropped and the divers will be allowed to plead guilty to the smaller charges. Even that will mean some years in prison."

"Yamura-Gonda," Bob went on, "is being returned to Japan. He'll go to prison for fraud, and maybe for a lot of other crimes, too. Torao's father has already been named president of the Yamura Company, and he and Torao are going to try to undo the damage Gonda did to the company all these years. They're also going to place a monument to Shozo Yamura in the Yamura family burial ground."

"His just tribute after so many years of silence," Mr. Hitchcock said. "And does the protest sail continue? Will the oil company drill?"

"Mr. MacGruder decided to oppose Hanley openly," Jupiter reported. "He went to the company's board of directors and told them that the drilling shouldn't start until more safeguards are installed. Mr. Hanley was furious, but the board backed MacGruder! So the protest has really won, but we should also get the oil we need!"

"A satisfying conclusion," Mr. Hitchcock decided.

"Then you will introduce the case?" Bob said.

"Not so fast, young man! I'm really quite worn out by all your exploits. You might give me a rest!" He chuckled when he saw the boys' stricken expressions. "All right, lads. I'll introduce your case—if you can satisfy me on two points! First, was Jupiter's identification of the diver before he removed his mask only a fortunate guess? It would seem so!"

Jupiter was insulted. "In no way, sir! When we were hiding from Yamura and the Connors brothers, I realized that the diver wasn't working with Yamura but against him! That was why they sank the motorboat even though the diver could still have been under it. And that's why Yamura spied on Mr. Crowe's house, and why the Connors brothers searched the *Sea Wind*. That search puzzled me—if the diver was in league with the Connors brothers, they would have known what he was up to on the *Sea Wind*—but then I realized that they were looking for signs of the diver! Since it was Mr. Crowe's house that

Yamura spied on, and I recalled that Mr. Crowe had mentioned Torao's name at the wharf, it had to be Torao they were after!"

"Very well," Mr. Hitchcock conceded grumpily. "A good deduction. But explain to me how Torao returned to shore that first day when he missed the *Sea Wind!* He could only attach to the *Sea Wind,* and yet there was no other time the boat ran short of fuel! Answer me that, and I will introduce the case. Hah! Admit it, Master Jones, for once you are stumped!"

"No, sir, it is really quite simple." Jupiter grinned. "Torao spent the night on Santa Cruz and rode back under the *Sea Wind* the very next day! But that wasn't one of the days that Captain Jason noticed a fuel shortage. The extra weight on the return trip wasn't enough to prevent the boat from reaching Santa Barbara." He became thoughtful. "As with the ring, sir, it was another case of human nature. People tend to be observant only when things go wrong! At sea, Captain Jason was concerned about having enough fuel to return to shore, so he watched his fuel gauge. But on the day after the first shortage, the fuel level was normal when the return trip began. It was very low when the boat reached the harbor, but that seemed normal for the end of the day. So the captain simply never noticed the shortage of fuel that trip!"

"Thunderation!" Mr. Hitchcock groaned. "The insufferable boy has done it again! You shall have your introduction."

As the boys laughed, Pete took an object from a bag he was holding. It was the steel box with the emblem of the Japanese Imperial Navy, which had held the sunken sub's logbook. Pete showed it to Mr. Hitchcock.

"We thought you might like to see this, sir," he said. "Torao gave it to us as a souvenir of the case."

"Impressive!" said the director. "But you should really repair the lock. Vandalism is so unsightly!" He laughed as Pete flushed. "One more question. What has Mr. John Crowe gained from the adventure?"

"Oh," Bob said, "he thinks he'll write a book about it!"

"Ah, yes, an author turns every experience into a book! You must make haste to beat him, my young friends!"

Grinning, the famous director watched the boys file out of his office and wondered what exhausting adventures they'd become embroiled in next!

THE THREE INVESTIGATORS
MYSTERY SERIES